# the House

## jasmine watkins

**The House**

*A Millennial's Deliverance*

by Jasmine Watkins

©2023, Jasmine Watkins

jasminehowell09@gmail.com

Published by Anointed Fire™ House

www.anointedfirehouse.com

Cover Design by Damascus Media

ISBN: 978-1-955557-45-0

# DEDICATIONS

*hearts of all those who knew and loved you. Rest in peace, Mom. I love you more than you will ever know.*

*With all my love,*

*Jasmine Watkins*

---

**To my beloved husband, Devin, and my three beautiful children Are, Wonder, and Onor:**

*This book would not have been possible without your unwavering love and support. You have been my constant companions on this journey, cheering me on through the long hours of writing and providing me with the inspiration and motivation I needed to keep going.*

*Devin, you have been my partner in life and in love, my best friend, and my soulmate. Your unwavering belief in me and your tireless support has been the bedrock of our family, and I am forever grateful for the love and joy you bring into my life each and every day.*

*Are, Wonder, and Onor, you are the lights of my life, the reason for everything I do. Your boundless energy, your curiosity, and your zest for life inspire me every day, and I am so blessed to be your mother. Watching you grow, learn and discover the world around you fills me with a sense of wonder and awe, and I* am constantly amazed by the love and compassion you show to others.

This book is dedicated to all of you, my beloved family, because you are the ones who make my life worth living. You are my everything, my reason for being, and I am so grateful to have you by my side on this incredible journey called life.

With all my love,

Neek, Mommy

---

## To my fellow Millennials:

This book is for us. It is a testament to the strength, resilience, and creativity of our generation. We have faced unprecedented challenges in our lives - economic uncertainty, political turmoil, social unrest - but through it all, we have refused to be defeated.

We are a generation that is not content to accept the status quo. We know that there is a better way, a more just and equitable way, and we are committed to doing whatever it takes to make that vision a reality.

Our assignment is clear: to cast out devils, to break the generational curses that have held us and our families back for far too long, and to advance the Kingdom of God through the power of the arts. We are artists, writers, musicians, dancers, filmmakers - and we know that our creativity is a powerful force for change.

This book is a call to action. It is a reminder that we are not alone in our struggles, and that together, we can overcome even the greatest obstacles. Let us continue to fight for justice, to speak truth to power, and to use our gifts and talents to build a better world for ourselves and for future generations.

To my fellow Millennials, I dedicate this book to you. May it inspire you, encourage you, and empower you to fulfill your destiny and change the world.

With hard work, hope, and determination, we can be the agents of change that this world needs.

Jasmine Watkins

# TABLE OF CONTENTS

# INTRODUCTION

BOOM! BOOM! BOOM! The sound of obnoxious knocking echoes throughout the house, and because the old wooden door had been through so much, it was barely hanging on the hinges. From the back of the house, which is where Cynthia's room was, a loud angry voice cried out,

"HELLO!" she yells.
"Who is it now?" Cynthia grumbles as she makes her way to the door.

No one responds back, so with her back slightly turned away from the door, Cynthia slowly turns the doorknob, yanks it open, and continues to head back to her room without looking to see who is at the door.

As Cynthia walks away, she starts to whisper under her breath, "I am so tired. I'm not in the mood for company right now."

She does not notice that there is no one at the

door. The door was left open because Cynthia refused to turn around and acknowledge whoever was at the door after she'd opened it. She walks through the front room and turns the corner to head back to her room. The wooden floor in the hallway creaks as she takes each dreadful step. Cynthia goes into her room, shuts the door, and lies on her bed in the dark. "Maybe, it's time for me to get out of the house," mumbles Cynthia. "I need to go to church, visit my mother, or maybe I should just go to my closet and talk to God. I'm tired of dealing with these depressing emotions. I need help!" cries Cynthia.

Cynthia's mother has been in the hospital for weeks now because she just had surgery on her leg due to her diabetes. Cynthia just wants life to be over with at this point. She is tired of dealing with trauma and mood swings.

There is a dark cloud of heaviness that follows her wherever she goes. Darkness seems to be connected to her. Every time darkness knocks, she answers. Every time trouble knocks, she answers. Every time life hits her hard, she falls down and refuses to get up. Cynthia's mental house was full of childhood demons and traumatic generational events. The doors were always being knocked on, kicked down, and broken into. It was truly a place of constant invasion.

## Welcome to The House.

# THE SPIRIT OF REJECTION

*The spirit of rejection is a powerful force that can have a profound impact on a person's life. It can cause feelings of worthlessness, insecurity, and inadequacy, and can lead to a range of negative behaviors, including substance abuse, self-harm, and even suicide. In the Bible, rejection is a common theme, and there are many examples of individuals who have struggled with the spirit of rejection and overcame it through faith and trust in God.*

*One of the most prominent examples of rejection in the Bible is the story of Joseph. Joseph was the favored son of his father, Jacob, which caused jealousy and resentment among his brothers. They sold him into slavery, and he ended up in Egypt, where he was falsely accused of a crime and thrown into prison. Despite these setbacks, Joseph never lost faith in God and eventually rose to become the second most powerful man in Egypt, eventually using his position to save his family from a severe famine that plagued the land at that time.*

*Another example of rejection in the Bible is the story of David. David was the youngest son of Jesse, and his older brothers looked down on him because of his youth and inexperience. When the prophet, Samuel, came to anoint the next king of Israel, David's brothers were all passed over, and David was chosen. Despite his youth and lack of experience, David went on to become one of the greatest kings in Israel's history, known for his faith, courage, and leadership.*

*The Bible teaches us that the spirit of rejection is not from God, but from the enemy. In 1 Peter 5:8, we are warned to "be sober-minded; be watchful." In this scripture, God goes on to say, "Your adversary the devil prowls around like a roaring lion, seeking someone to devour." The devil wants to use rejection to destroy us, but God has given us the power to overcome it through faith in His Son, Jesus Christ.*

*In John 1:12, we read, "But to all who did receive him, who believed in his name, he gave the right to become children of God." When we accept Jesus as our Savior and believe in*

*His name, we become children of God, with all the privileges and blessings that come with that status. We are no longer slaves to the spirit of rejection, but are instead heirs to the Kingdom of God.*

*In Romans 8:31, we read, "What then shall we say to these things? If God is for us, who can be against us?" When we put our faith in God, we can be confident that He is with us and will never leave us nor forsake us. We may face rejection and persecution in this world, but we can take comfort in the knowledge that we are loved and accepted by God.*

*Rejection gives you a broken lens in life. You only see what rejection wants you to see and hear what it wants you to hear. It doesn't play fair at all.*

# CHAPTER 1

## WELCOME REJECTED R.J.

*Rejection is one of the most prevalent issues that makes its way into the womb to be passed down from one generation to the next. It takes a renewal of the mind, body and soul to get rid of the feeling of being rejected. Rejection is an open door in itself. It opens the door to many other issues. Rejection opens the door to every issue found under the sun, and it often starts with a conversation with a parent.*

In a small brick two-bedroom home on Wirt Avenue in Portsmouth, Virginia, lived a small, beautiful family of three by the name of the Copeland's. It was always just the three of them together—family vacations, holidays, birthdays, and summer fun all included.

Ruth is a 33-year old, brown-skinned mother of two kids named Cynthia and Andre. Ruth has thick, jet black hair that flows midways down her back. Her son, Andre, is eleven-years old, while Cynthia is seven. Ruth calls them the seven-eleven siblings named, of course, after her favorite store. The Seven-Eleven is just a few blocks from their home. Ruth is a hardworking single mother who works extra long hours at the United State Postal Service to raise her children.

The Post Office takes up the majority of Ruth's life. It's a big, cold warehouse with a hard concrete floor and loud machines constantly working. Some days, she has to go to work at 2:30 in the morning, and she gets off at three the following afternoon. Ruth always left Cynthia and Andre at home because she cannot rely on or trust anyone to babysit her children. She has very bad trust issues because life has not always been good to her. Ruth's mother was seventy-years old and very sick; she was always in and out of the emergency room. The doctors would always tell the family that her heart would give out any day or at any given moment. Ruth was the fifth child born out of six siblings. Her siblings would never get along with one another because Ruth was the responsible one. Anytime someone needed something, they called on Ruth and she would come to the rescue, but the favor was never returned. The grandmother was the glue that held the family together.

On a nice breezy cloudy day in Portsmouth, there were always fun shenanigans and craziness happening all at once. There was never an in-between. Either you would hear the joyful, yet loud children laughing, playing, and running around outside or you would hear gunshots, yelling, and the screams of the bitter neighbors who did not get along with one another. The streets smelled like old trash and dirty drugs. There was a big green house on the corner that always had a lot of visitors, along with a bunch of old cars that were parked in the front yard.

Ruth's house was different in so many ways. It was the only small brick house on the street, and it always seemed quiet during the day and peaceful at night. Life at the Copeland's was pretty simple, but there were a lot of unrevealed, hidden secrets even the children would never want to open up to one another about. Cynthia was the quiet, shy one out of the two. She was always smiling, laughing, and thinking about something creative to do. She thought of herself as the weird one who stuck out like a sore thumb.

*Cynthia places her small hands to her mouth to project her voice.*

"MAAAA!" yells the seven-year-old girl with the thick, curly hair and brown skin that glistened like the sun, but *with Cynthia's squeaky little voice, no one could hear her.*

She takes off running to the back room where her mother is to get her attention.

*Ruth is blasting her favorite 'Yolanda Adams in concert' VHS tape. She is in her worship zone.* "WHAT, Bookie?" Ruth answers in a frustrated tone.

"I'm bored. Can I go outside?" asks little Cynthia. "Go outside? It is six in the evening; you don't need to go worrying folks! Go sit down somewhere and leave me alone," Ruth shouts while running out of breath. Her shortness of breath is due to the fact that she's been singing and shouting to her favorite concert tape that is playing loudly in the room.

*Cynthia folds her arms and pouts her little lips.*

"Uggh! I can never go nowhere," shouts the sad, rejected little girl. Cynthia runs off with her tiny feet stomping down the hallway so her mother can hear.

*Every step of the little girl's feet irritates the mother and reminds her of animals running in the house.*

"NO running in my house! You better stop before you really can't go anywhere else!" yells Ruth.

This was a normal day for Cynthia. Andre is

pretty chill and keeps to himself a lot. He is always listening to his music and playing video games in his room right across the hall from Ruth's room. Andre's room smells like old gym socks and sweaty football players. So, Cynthia rarely goes in there unless she is really bored. Cynthia doesn't have her own room so she shares the bed with her mother or, at times, she likes to sleep in the front room, which they called the den. Cynthia calls it her room, since her mother and brother have their own rooms. She needs a getaway as well. It's her imaginary playhouse. She is pretty mature for a seven-year old. Well, at least she thinks so.

Cynthia likes to hide in the closet in the den whenever she is upset with her mother or brother. She always hides in there until she cries herself to sleep or after praying to God. She has a very close relationship with God. No one understands her the way God, her heavenly Father, does.

*Cynthia places her hands together and gets on her little knees as she prays every day in the small crowded closet.*

"God, I know I am not supposed to talk back to mommy, but I was very angry at her for yelling at me when I did nothing wrong. She is always yelling at me, calling me mean names, and I don't understand why. God, can you help mommy to be nicer to me? Can you let my grandma live longer so I can live with her? In Jesus name, AMEN!" With tears pouring from her little sparkly black eyes, she whispers softly in the closet. She then gets up to go into the den to watch television. She does this until she falls asleep.

Ruth comes out of her room and sees Cynthia in the den sleeping. She walks up to her, picks her up, and carries her to the bedroom. This is an everyday routine for Ruth. She comes home, makes dinner, and watches television on the wooden big screen TV in her room. She would do this while getting her things ready for work in the morning. After she gets her things ready, she gets the kids ready for bed and spends time with God right beside her queen-sized, gold-framed bed.

Getting her rest, prayer time and productivity is what Ruth lives for. Being a single mother, life often gets hectic for her, but she never lets it show. Ruth is a tough-hearted, emotionless, and yet, sweetheart of a woman at times. She knows exactly when to turn her feelings on and when to turn them off. This is why it was so easy for her to divorce her ex-husband, who happens to be the father of Cynthia and Andre. Ruth had Andre when she was married, but she had Cynthia after the couple split up. Ruth's ex-husband's name is Frank. No one really likes to speak much about him. The children don't see him much anymore; this is ever since a big crazy fight happened between him and Ruth. The last time Cynthia saw her father was when she was three-years old. Therefore, she doesn't have many memories of him, except the way he inappropriately touched her every time he visited. She calls him Pete because she doesn't want to call him Daddy. The name Pete is a name of a creepy character that Andre watches on one of his favorite shows. Anytime her brother steals the remote, Cynthia covers her eyes.

Ruth can never forgive herself for having a child out of wedlock. That is also how Cynthia felt; she felt like she was a mistake. She believed that she was the child that everyone wishes had never been born. All the same, Ruth clearly never released those emotions to anyone, but it definitely shows in the way she favors Andre. When Andre calls his mother, Ruth answers, "Yes, baby?" But, when Cynthia calls her, Ruth answers with an annoyed attitude. "What, Bookie?!"

She covers up her disdain for her daughter by using the nickname Bookie, but Cynthia can hear the difference in her tone and always feels rejected by her mother. Cynthia is a very emotional child and she can discern really well. She is always telling people how they feel and she pays very close attention to the actions of others. She does this to the point where she will know so much about a person based on her detailed observations. Everyone thinks

Cynthia is strange and different. She can never fit in anywhere she goes.

# THE SPIRIT OF DECEIT

Deceit is a common tactic of the enemy, and it is something that Christians must guard themselves against. The Bible warns us that Satan is a deceiver, and he will do everything in his power to lead us astray. The spirit of deceit is a powerful force that can take hold in a person's life and cause that person to stray from the truth.

In John 8:44, Jesus tells the Pharisees, "You are of your father, the devil, and the desires of your father you want to do. He was a murderer from the beginning, and does not stand in the truth, because there is no truth in him. When he speaks a lie, he speaks from his own resources, for he is a liar and the father of it." This verse makes it clear that Satan is the father of lies and that his goal is to deceive us.

The spirit of deceit can manifest in many ways. It can come in the form of false teachings, false prophets, and false doctrines. In 2 Corinthians 11:13-15, Paul warns the Corinthians about false apostles, saying, "For such are false apostles, deceitful workers, transforming themselves into apostles of Christ. And no wonder! For Satan himself transforms himself into an angel of light. Therefore it is no great thing if his ministers also transform themselves into ministers of righteousness, whose end will be according to their works."

The spirit of deceit can also manifest in our own hearts and minds. It can cause us to lie, cheat, and deceive others, as well as ourselves. In Psalm 32:2, David writes, "Blessed is the man to whom the Lord does not impute iniquity, and in whose spirit there is no deceit." This verse reminds us that we must guard our hearts and minds against the spirit of deceit and seek God's truth in all things.

Breaking free from the spirit of deceit requires a willingness to confront our own hearts and minds and seek God's truth above all else. In John 14:6, Jesus says, "I am the way, the truth, and the life. No one comes to the Father except through Me." This verse reminds us that Jesus is the truth and that we must follow Him above all else.

We must guard our hearts and minds against the spirit of deceit and seek God's truth above all else. By following Jesus and seeking His truth, we can *break free from the spirit of deceit and live a life of freedom and truth.*

# CHAPTER 2

## HELLO? WHO'S THERE?

*Knock! Knock! Knock!* The sound of loud knocking terrifies everyone in the house. Three people yell out at the same time, "Who's there?" "It's me! R.J. again!" says the person behind the door.
"Come in," yells Red.

R.J. places his hand on the knob and slowly opens the door. Behind R.J. are several people following him.

"Hey, you guys, I'm back! I know I have been gone for a while, but you knew I wouldn't be gone for long. This is my home! No matter how many times I leave, I will always find a way back in," says R.J. Curious and calmly, Red responds, "Oh, it's cool. Come sit down and introduce us to your friends that I see you have brought with you this time around."

Red is the mind of the house and the ringleader of the crew, so no one comes into the house unless Red knows who and why they are there. With long, fiery red hair and blue eyes, Red is the brain of the house because everyone has to go through him to get in.

The house is the mental reality of Cynthia Copeland. In fact, it's Cynthia's actual life in one place. Every encounter or traumatic event has built the house that these people have gathered at. R.J. came into the house when Cynthia was born. He is a generational issue that has not been handled in the previous generations before Cynthia. When someone enters the house, they are entering into the life of Cynthia. Many have forced themselves in, while some were given access by events and even impactful or hurtful conversations. R.J. comes in every time Cynthia feels rejected or unwanted. Red is Cynthia's best friend and her closest loved one. He is attached to this place. When anyone enters, he will open the door. He has the keys and the locks to all of the entrances.

R.J. flops on the couch, kicks his feet up and lets out a long sigh. "Whew, there is no place like home." Red and his friends continue to discuss their topic regarding who the next person to return will be.

"I think Pete is going to return next because Cyn hasn't been around her father in a while, and he may show up soon," says Hannah. "Well, maybe he will come around soon because the holidays are slowly approaching," R.J. quietly responds as he doses off to sleep with his big, hairy hands hanging off of the black leather couch. Red is sitting across from his friends in his tall, silver, royal chair. The room is getting almost pitch dark because the curtains have been closed all day, so Red turns on the lamp and asks R.J. why he's going to sleep when he hasn't introduced his friends yet.

"Why do I have to introduce them? They know how to introduce themselves," R.J. complains. The lady with the blue hair starts to chuckle and says, "My name is Charlotte."

"Hi, Charlotte," says Red. "What brings you to the house?" Red asks as he places his glasses on a wooden desk.

"I came with R.J. He asked me if I wanted to come here and meet his friends, so I told him yes," Charlotte answers.

"Oh, okay; cool," Red says with a grin on his face. "Why are you smiling?" Charlotte asks.

"You don't remember me, Charlotte?" Red asks.

"No, I don't recall. Where would I remember you from?" Charlotte answers with a smirk without Red looking. When Red looks her way, Charlotte pauses, rubs her head, and puts a puzzled look on her face.

"Just think a little harder. You know exactly how," says Red.


Red does not have time to go back and forth with Charlotte's deceitful ways, so he walks away and heads to the kitchen where the six other guests are so he can go and play detective with them as well. Red loves having the upper hand in every situation. He knows everything that takes place and he loves to pick anyone's brain that has one.

In the kitchen is where all of the fun is being had. People are at the table playing cards, and by the island counter, there is a huge debate going on between Robin and Sal. Robin is another long-term guest in the house. Robin, Pete, Red, and R.J. know each other very well. They all came into the house when Cynthia was at a young age, except for R.J. and Red; they basically helped build the house. Red and R.J. have a special relationship and are basically the big bullies of the house. Red runs the show and R.J. is the main event of the show.

"Robin! You didn't come to the house until Cyn met her friend in preschool," Sal forcefully yells. Robin sarcastically answers, "No, of course not, Sal. I came when Cyn was five-years old after she had a play date with the daughter of her mother's friend. You do not know what you're talking about, Sal."

Robin and Sal can never get along. Robin is the rebellious one. Sal has to be the right, snaky one.

"How did you come when she was two if I came when she was six? You weren't here that much longer than me," Sal says.

"Tell me why this matters again? No, never mind that question. I'm done talking to you! *Humph!*," Robin snarls as she flips her hair and crosses her arms.

"Ha ha ha! I get so much joy in listening to you two make a fool of yourselves. You two should grow up one day. Maybe, one day, I will walk in and see you guys having an adult, civilized conversation," Red says as he rests his hands on Robin and Sal's shoulders.

"Don't touch me, Red," says Robin.

"Oh, poor foolish girl. I remember when you came to the house. It was the day Cyn was rebellious and sneaky for the first time in her life during a play date. You came knocking on the door, and who let you in?" Red asks.

"You did," Robin answers as she rolls her eyes and walks toward the front room where R.J. is still napping.

The house has new people moving into it everyday, but the familiar ones never want to leave. They have called this place home for years; some for even generations. Red keeps things under control. He even kicks people out who try to overstay their visits. R.J. keeps getting kicked out, but he seems to always find his way back. He left one day after Cyn found the confidence to tell him to go.
Cyn has the authority and power to kick people out, but she always finds a way to give access back to the ones that left.

# THE SPIRIT OF REBELLION

*The spirit of rebellion is a powerful force that can lead to chaos, destruction, and ultimately, separation from God. It is a spirit that has been present throughout human history, and has caused countless individuals and nations to turn away from God to pursue their own selfish desires. In the Bible, rebellion is a common theme, and there are many examples of individuals who have succumbed to its powers and suffered the consequences.*

*One of the most well-known examples of rebellion in the Bible can be found in the story of Adam and Eve. They were created by God and placed in the Garden of Eden, with only one commandment to follow: not to eat from the tree of the knowledge of good and evil. But they were tempted by the serpent, and in an act of rebellion, they ate from the tree, disobeying God's commandment. This act of rebellion led to their expulsion from the Garden and brought sin and death into the world.*

*Another example of rebellion in the Bible is the story of the Israelites. They were chosen by God to be His people, and were led out of slavery in Egypt* by Moses. But despite God's many blessings and miracles, the Israelites repeatedly rebelled against Him, grumbling and complaining about their circumstances and longing to return to Egypt. Their rebellion ultimately led to forty years of wandering in the wilderness, and only a remnant of them were allowed to enter the promised land.

The Bible teaches us that rebellion is a sin, and that it ultimately leads to separation from God. In 1 Samuel 15:23, we read, "For rebellion is as the sin of witchcraft, and stubbornness is as iniquity and idolatry." Rebellion is not simply a matter of disobeying God's commands, but is a rejection of His authority and a desire to pursue our own selfish desires.

In Romans 13:1-2, we read, "Let every soul be subject to the governing authorities. For there is no authority except from God, and the authorities that exist are appointed by God. Therefore whoever resists the authority resists the ordinance of God, and those who resist will bring judgment on themselves." God has ordained the authorities that exist in this world, and we are called to submit to them. This does not mean that we blindly obey every command, but rather that we recognize that *all authority ultimately comes from God.*

*The spirit of rebellion is a powerful force that can lead us away from God and towards destruction. As believers, we are called to submit to God's authority, and to recognize that all authority ultimately comes from Him. We must resist the temptation to pursue our own selfish desires, and instead seek to follow God's will for our lives. By doing so, we can avoid the consequences of rebellion and enjoy the blessings of obedience and faithfulness.*

# CHAPTER 3

## REBELLIOUS ROBIN

Rebellion is an attitude. Disobedience is an act, but it is connected to rebellion when it is under authority. Rebellion is when you disobey authority. Many acts of disobedience will result from the character of rebellion. Cynthia welcomed rebellion in by completing an act of disobedience. Even if it is done in innocence, access is given to this spirit through guilty or shameful thoughts that are pondered.

It was June 26th, 1999, the day before Cynthia turned five-years old. It was a Saturday and a windy, breezy day in Virginia. Ruth finally had an off day, so she scheduled a play date with her very good friend, Carly, and her daughter, Brooke.

That day, Cynthia was four-years old, still very shy and very curious, meaning she was always asking questions and wanting to know about new things.

As Ruth and five-year old, Cynthia, walks up to the beautiful red double-doors that led to Mrs. Carly's five-bedroom, stone home, she asks Ruth, "Mommy, why can't we have a house like this?"
"Because I am your only parent," Ruth answers.
"So, what does that have to do with having a big house....?"
"Hey, ladies!" says Mrs. Carly.

Their conversation is interrupted by the door opening. In walks a gorgeous, tall, red-headed woman with fair skin and blue eyes. Ruth is so grateful because she doesn't want to answer any more of Cynthia's curiosity-driven questions.

"Hey, girl. How are you?"
Ruth responds in a tired, worn out tone,
"I'm great. Come on in; let me take your jackets and your purse," Mrs. Carly says politely.

It is a windy day outside, even though it is 80 degrees; the wind is very strong and breezy, so jackets were needed if you were outside that summer day. Ruth hands her jacket and purse to Mrs. Carly.

"Let's go to the living room and catch up while the girls go play in Brooke's room," Mrs. Carly says.
"Brooke! Cynthia is here!" Mrs. Carly yells.
"Go ahead, pretty girl. She should be in her room. You know where to go."

*Before Cynthia can open up her mouth to say anything, the sound of little feet running on the hardwood floors of the hallway echoes throughout the house.*

Carly's daughter has just turned six and she indeed has a very dominating and bossy attitude. Brooke can get anyone to listen to her, including Cynthia, or as Brooke calls her, "my little Cynnie." She said this as if Cynthia is that much younger than her, but at any cost, Brooke wants to feel like she is in control, so she gives all of her friends little nicknames that make her feel like she is their boss.

*Brooke runs out of her room, heads to the front with so much excitement, and grabs Cynthia by the hand.*

"Hi, my little Cynnie! Oh my gosh! I love your shoes! I had some like those, ummm maybe when I was a year old. Ha! That was so long ago. Anyway, come on! I have so many new toys to show you!"

*You can tell by the look on Cynthia's face that she is very excited and very nervous at the same time.*

In her little squeaky voice, Cynthia responds, "Hi, Brooke! Sure, let's go," as if she has a choice in the matter. While Brooke is running and pulling her into her big beautiful pink bedroom, Cynthia falls down and hurts her little knees.

*Cynthia tries to get up off the floor, but she*

*stops to look at her left knee. She then grabs her knee after she sees a small scrape on it.*

"OUCH!" screams little Cynthia.

"My knee hurts really bad! Mommy! Mommy!" Cynthia dramatically yells.
"Oh, I am so sorry, my little Cynnie. Don't call your mommy. You will be just fine," Brooke says.

*Cynthia loves playing with Brooke and never can say no to the short, bossy, little red-headed girl.*

Cynthia hops right up, and with her little hands, she rubs her eyes and starts following Brooke to her bedroom. The smell of vanilla cookies and cake fill Cynthia's nostrils as she walks into the room. Brooke's room is every little girl's dream. She has every dollhouse you can think of and every shade of pink to ever exist can be found on the walls to the bed and even the carpet. You can only imagine just how spoiled this little girl is.

"Hey, my little Cynnie. Come to my closet. I want to show you something," says Brooke.
*Cynthia walks over to the closet.*
Curious, Cynthia asks, "Whoa! Where did you get that big piggy bank from, and how did you get all of those quarters?"
Brooke responds with a smirk on her face, "I took them from my mommy and daddy's cars, and some of my friends at school brought me some from their parents as well."

*Little Cynthia didn't really understand that she was stealing from everyone; she just thought it was very cool looking.*

"But shhh, don't tell your mommy or brother. It's our little secret," Brooke whispers as she bends over closer to little Cynthia.
"Okay, I won't," Cynthia responds. "But what will you do with all of those quarters and pennies?"
"Oh, I'm going to save it for when the ice cream truck comes or when my cousin takes me to the store with her," replies Brooke.
"But I thought you weren't allowed to go with

your cousin anymore since she told you to take something from the store," Cynthia says.

"Mind your own business, please and thank you," Brooke says with an attitude because she knows that Cynthia is right.

"Okay, my mouth is sealed. Can we go play with your dollhouses now?" Cynthia asks.

"Sure, but first, you have to go get me some quarters from your mother's purse. I never let anyone touch my dollhouses without bringing me quarters. It's only fair; right?" Brooke snottily states.

Cynthia knows that she is not allowed to go into her mommy's purse, but she really wants to play with Brooke, so she doesn't mind being rebellious if it means she can play with those life-sized dollhouses.

Little Cynthia heads into the front room where her mommy and Mrs. Carly are. Both Mrs. Carly and Ruth look at Cynthia and wonder why she is just standing there smiling.

*Cynthia does not know how to go about*

*committing her very first crime, so she just stands there looking innocent in her cute little blue dress and curly long pigtails.*

"Mommy, can I go to the bathroom?" Cynthia asks.
"Bookie, you know where the bathroom is. Go ahead," Ruth answers.

Cynthia walks nervously down the hallway where she'd seen the coats and her mommy's purse hanging up by the door. Cynthia grabs her mommy's purse and runs into the bathroom with it. As she opens the purse, it has so many compartments, she doesn't know where her mommy keeps her quarters.

She searches and finally finds a small pouch where she hears a lot of jingling and rattling. She grabs as many quarters as she can and stuffs them in the little pockets of her dress. She is so scared that her mommy will catch her that she hurries up and puts the purse back by her jacket. She then takes off running quietly back to Brooke's room. With every step she takes, her heart races even faster than when she was running.

"Finally! I was worried you got caught or something," Brooke says.

*Little Cynthia's heart is still beating fast. She wants to go home to her little closet and talk to God about taking from her mommy. She doesn't want Brooke to know, so she keeps her head down in shame.*

"No, I didn't get caught, but it was too close. Whew, I don't think I can do that again, Brooke," Cynthia says.

"Well, my Little Cynnie, you are growing up! Now, you have earned your playtime with my dolls and my dollhouses."

*Cynthia wasn't in the mood to play anymore, but she didn't want to disappoint her friend, Brooke, so she put on a smile and played with her dollhouse.*

"Okay, let's go play," sighs Cynthia.

Little Cynthia and Brooke play for hours and

hours until they are worn out and fall asleep on Brooke's pretty pink princess bed.

"Bookie! It's time to go!" Ruth yells down the long, glamorous, wooden-walled hallway from the all-white linen front room. Cynthia and Brooke are still sound asleep, so there is no response.

*Ruth quickly gets up with frustration. She has a bit of an issue with being patient, especially when she is ready to leave. She walks down the hallway with her black leather boots cackling on the wooden floors. When she arrives at Brooke's room, she notices that the two little girls are asleep and wrapped up in pink, puffy covers, but she doesn't care. She is ready to go. All the same, she is in a rush to go and pick up Andre from football practice.*

"Wake up, Cynthia. We have to go, Bookie. Go put on your shoes and jacket, and meet me in the front."

*Cynthia slowly stretches and yawns while*

*rubbing her eyes. She steps down from the high bed with her little feet and reaches for her shoes.*

"Okay, mommy, I'm coming," says Cynthia in her little, raspy and sleepy voice. Cynthia meets her mother at the front door. She grabs her hand and opens the door while saying her goodbyes to Mrs. Carly.

"See you next time, Miss Lady. I will call you after I get settled in to finish our conversation. Let me go get this boy before he drives me crazy. I'm already late. Thanks again for the play date. I'm sure Cynthia had fun," Ruth says.

"Alright, ladies. Don't forget to call me, Ruth!" Mrs. Carly responds as she smiles and waves.

Ruth and Cynthia walk to the purple van before entering it; they then head to pick up Andre from practice.

"Mommy, I love you and I'm sorry if I never show it," Cynthia cries.

*Ruth looks up in the rear-view mirror and notices Little Cynthia is crying and wiping her eyes.*

"What's the matter, Bookie?" Ruth calmly asks.
"Oh, nothing. I'm just tired and sleepy," Cynthia whispers.
"Are you sure, you crybaby?" Ruth chuckles.
"Yes, mommy," Cynthia answers.

# STRONGHOLD SPIRIT

The term "stronghold" is used in the Bible to refer to a place of refuge or a place of protection. In the spiritual sense, a stronghold can refer to a negative thought pattern or a sin that has taken root in a person's life and has become a "stronghold." Strongholds are difficult to overcome. The Bible speaks of the need to tear down these strongholds and replace them with the truth of God's Word.

In 2 Corinthians 10:4-5, the apostle Paul writes, "For the weapons of our warfare are not carnal but mighty in God for pulling down strongholds, casting down arguments and every high thing that exalts itself against the knowledge of God, bringing every thought into captivity to the obedience of Christ." Paul is speaking here of the need to fight against the spiritual forces that are opposed to God and His truth. He recognizes that these forces can take hold in a person's life and become a stronghold that is difficult to break free from.

One of the most common strongholds that people struggle with is fear. Fear can become a stronghold when it becomes a dominant thought pattern that shapes a person's worldview and behavior. In Psalm 27:1, the psalmist writes, "The Lord is my light and my salvation; whom shall I fear? The Lord is the strength of my life; of whom shall I be afraid?" This verse reminds us that God is our stronghold and that we can find refuge in Him when we are struggling with fear.

Another common stronghold is addiction. Addiction can take hold in a person's life and become a dominant force that is difficult to overcome. In 1 Corinthians 6:12, Paul writes, "All things are lawful for me, but all things are not helpful. All things are lawful for me, but I will not be brought under the power of any." This verse reminds us that we must be careful not to allow anything to take control of our lives and become a stronghold that we cannot break free from.

Breaking free from strongholds requires a willingness to confront our own thoughts and behaviors and to seek God's help in overcoming them. In Isaiah 26:3, we read, "You will keep him in perfect peace, whose mind is stayed on You, because he trusts in You." This verse reminds us that when we keep our minds focused on God and His truth, we can find the peace and strength we *need to break free from strongholds.*

*In conclusion, strongholds are negative thought patterns or sins that can take hold in a person's life and become a dominant force that is difficult to overcome. The Bible teaches us that we must tear down these strongholds and replace them with the truth of God's Word. By keeping our minds focused on God and His truth, we can find the strength we need to overcome strongholds and live the abundant life that God has planned for us.*

# CHAPTER 4

## THE MOOD ROOM

We all have that place in our lives where our emotions have become the ruler of our decisions. Your mind has thoughts, your heart has emotions, and your feelings have actions. The mood room can be described as Red's sanctuary or his palace; it can also be described as Cynthia's brain and heart. Red can play around with her thoughts, words, and even her feelings. The mood room without Red is more like the heart without emotions. It has to work together. Anyone that enters the house wants access to the mood room because it has a special glow to it. Red will not let this happen. He sometimes would lose access when Cynthia didn't let her feelings control her actions. The mood room would be locked, but during Cynthia's most vulnerable moments, the mood room would be accessible only to Red. It was only one other person who would try to gain access without the authority to do so, and that was Jez.

*Red paces back and forth in the small brick home outside of a room that led to the front room. The front room is filled with frustration and anxiousness.*

"Wake up, R.J.!" Red screams with anger.

*R.J. is sound asleep, but he jumps up out of his nap with his heart beating fast.*

What, what, what did I do?" R.J. screams as he jumps up out of his nap.

"We have so much to do and you are napping!" Red responds.
"Chill man, I thought the house was on fire or something," R.J. answers.

Red loves to be in control. Anyway he can, he wants to boss someone around. Red has been in the house since the very beginning because he is Cynthia's mind and emotions. He gives access to anyone that knocks. Red never really sleeps. He is always up working and trying to figure out a way to control something or someone. He doesn't like seeing anyone sleeping or napping. Just like any boss or supervisor, if someone isn't working, Red reasons that they aren't needed.

"R.J., get up! We need to talk!" Red says in a frustrated tone.

*R.J. sits up from the black leather couch and places his long, steel toe wooden shoes on the floor and rubs his small, black squinted eyes.*

"Bro, I'm up!" R.J. responds with bass in his voice.

By this time R.J. and Red are both frustrated with each other.
"This better be important," R.J. mumbles under his breath.

Red is sitting at his desk typing away. He has his red fiery hair pulled back in a ponytail and his blue eyes gaze into the screen.

"Okay, what's going on, Red boy? "R.J. asks.

Red, never taking his eyes off the screen, responds, "Okay, so do you know the young lady with the short blue hair that came in the house with you this morning?"

"Charlotte, yes. What about her?" asks R.J.

"Well, she stated earlier that she doesn't remember me, but I'm positive that I have seen her before," Red says.

"Charlotte has been here before. She came here right after Robin came. I don't know how she doesn't remember," R.J. states.

"Oh, she remembers. She just has a motive that I'm trying to figure out," Red responds.

*Charlotte tiptoes in the front room and hides behind the tall wooden fireplace, but not close enough for the guys to see her enter the room.*

*She sticks her head out and places her hands on the brick tower that is connected to the fireplace. She tries to listen to the conversation that is going on about her, but her focus zooms into a room that is glowing blue down the hallway.*

"Oh wow, there it is—the room I have been trying to get into since my first visit to this crazy house," Charlotte murmurs to herself.

*She continues to whisper and think to herself out loud while still trying to focus on what the guys are talking about.*

"Hmm, how can I get to that room? Maybe I can get Red away from his desk long enough to figure it out," Charlotte thinks to herself.

*Charlotte then hears R.J. say her name so she directs her eyes to her left where R.J. is sitting in the front room to read his lips.*

"Okay, are we done talking about Charlotte? I know you didn't wake me up just for this." R.J.

gets up out of the chair with frustration. He is anxious to get away from Red.

He stands up and begins to head towards the bathroom, which is down the hallway on his right; this is right past the fireplace and entrance to the kitchen. He walks past the fireplace and sees something in the corner of his eyes. He slowly turns around and notices Charlotte hiding beside the fireplace. R.J. gives her a curious stare and shakes his head before continuing to walk to the bathroom.
"You people are extremely weird in this house," R.J. mumbles to himself.

Charlotte overhears R.J.'s whisper so she rolls her eyes. She swipes her blue, soft straight hair out of her eyes and peeks from behind the fireplace. She notices Red is still sitting at his desk. She starts to walk towards him intending to get in his head and inquire about what he and R.J. were talking about. Red looks up from his computer with his striking blue eyes and squints at Charlotte.

"Yes, how may I be of assistance to you?" asks Red.

Red knows that Charlotte has been listening the entire time, but he is so focused on figuring her out that he doesn't want to add more fuel to the fire.

"Have you figured out everything you need to know about me yet, since you are so very curious?" asks Charlotte sarcastically.

*Red pauses and realizes who Charlotte might be in his records. He still isn't quite sure, but he doesn't want Charlotte to know that he is second-guessing himself.*

"I figured you out when you walked in the door. I just want to know why you insisted on lying to me," Red responds.
"Lying is not the word I would use, but okay, I was here before, but I enjoy letting people discover more about me, rather than me telling them everything," Charlotte says as she blows on her long, pointy blue nails.

"Okay, well in my system, it notes that you were here in the house, but you weren't here for long. You seemed to have disappeared from my records after like a couple of hours of being here," Red says as he scrolls through the pages of data on his computer.

"Keep looking, you will find out. I had an interesting entrance and exit from this house." Charlotte smirks and begins to walk away in her three-inch black pumps.

*Charlotte wants Red to get all bothered about this so she can find a way to get to that room down the hallway.*

"Maybe Lacy can help me," Charlotte thinks to herself.

Charlotte walks through the front room and begins to scan the room to find her friend, Lacy. She is anxious to talk to Lacy about what had just happened with Red and herself. She starts to smile and giggle like a little schoolgirl who's ready to gossip to her friends.

In the kitchen, she finally spots Lacy sitting down talking to R.J., Robin, and Sal. Lacy has long, beautiful blondish white hair and red freckles. She is always twirling her flawless blonde hair with her skinny fingers whenever she is talking. Lacy is the flirty, lustful one. Charlotte and Lacy are the best of friends. Their personalities complement one another so well. Charlotte can deceive anyone and Lacy can manipulate anyone with her flirtatious ways.

*Charlotte taps Lacy on the shoulder to get her attention.*

"Hey, Lacy. There you are. Let me pull you aside for a sec," says Charlotte.
"Hey, Charlotte. Okay, come on; let's go outside," Lacy responds.

*Lacy gets up from the kitchen table, pushes the black metal chair in place, and tells the guys at the table that she will be right back.*

No one really pays attention to Lacy getting up from the table; they just continue their conversation without even noticing the girls leaving the kitchen.

Charlotte and Lacy look very suspicious as they slowly walk towards the back door in the kitchen. Charlotte places her hand on the door handle and begins to twist it. She then steps out on the porch.

"Lacy, it's kind of getting dark outside. Do you want to go back in or are you okay with the light being on?"

*Lacy doesn't like insects and Charlotte knows the light will attract the bugs outside if they turn it on. She doesn't want any interruptions because she knows her friend very well.*

"It is fine for now. I will step back inside if the nasty critters start to bother me," Lacy responds.

So, the two girls walk outside the back door of the kitchen. They then sit in the two red rocking chairs on the back porch. It is getting dark outside, but there is a bright light on the porch on top of the door. The breeze brushes against Lacy's long blonde hair as she crosses her legs in the wooden rocking chair.

*Lacy never misses a moment to fiddle her hair with her fingers as she talks and smirks.*

"So, what's going on, girly?" Lacy asks Charlotte.

"Lacy, so I think Red is figuring things out," Charlotte states.

"What?! Ha ha! I'm confused! Tell me more please," Lacy responds.

"Red has records of everyone who has entered the house and I am in it. We have to get to those records, Lacy. I can't let anyone find out my real name or how I came in here the first time," Charlotte explains.

*Charlotte has a history of deceiving everyone to the point where she has changed her name several times to reenter people's lives.*

"Lacy darling, do you think you can find out

how to get to that pretty shiny room right next to the bathroom?" Charlotte asks.

Curious, Lacy responds, "I don't know what room you are talking about, Hun, but maybe you should ask Red."

Charlotte knows that Lacy is innocent and oblivious to everything around her, but she can not take her blindness anymore.

"Lacy, why would I ask Red? You have to be joking with that dumb suggestion," Charlotte says as she rolls her eyes and shakes her head.

"Do you understand why I'm back again?" Charlotte asks.

Lacy is getting annoyed with all of the insects flying around her. Her attention span is very short, in addition to her not being very interested in what Charlotte has to say anymore.

"Okay, Hun. I'm going back inside. Let me know how everything goes," Lacy responds while huffing, puffing and waving her arms around trying to protect her flawlessly beautiful hair from the bugs outside.

"STUPID, NASTY BUGS!" Lacy yells while getting up from the rocking chair.

She quickly grabs the door handle and runs into the house where she is safe from nature and creatures. Still outside sitting on the back porch, Charlotte crosses her arms and lets out a big sigh.

"Ugh I don't know how I am going to get to that stupid mood room without Red figuring me out this time," Charlotte says to herself.

Charlotte doesn't understand how Red figured out she was here before because her name wasn't Charlotte when she was here years ago. Red is always aware of what is going on, but for some reason, he is out of the loop when it comes to Charlotte. He only has this frustration with one other person and Charlotte reminds him so much of her. She wanted to get to the mood room, but Red handled that problem years ago.

The mood room has too much control of Cyn for anyone to just come and mess it up. Anytime Cyn's mood changed, it was because Red was in the room rearranging things. He would randomly rearrange the color on the walls, buy new furniture, write words on things or just completely destroy the atmosphere in the room.

Cyn could be having a really amazing day, but after Red would enter the room and start painting the walls black, punching holes in the walls or writing doubtful and hateful words on the walls, Cynthia would start getting doubtful thoughts and crazy visions that would turn an awesome day into a chaotic one. This room is Red's sacred world. He can't control much without it. His favorite saying is, "If I can just be in control of her life, she would listen to everything I want her to do."

*Red is the emotions and the room is his*

*playground. Cyn lived by her emotions. Her emotions were in charge of her life, so therefore, Red is in charge of her life.*

The mood room has different colors on all four of the walls. These colors are determined by whatever mood Red decides he wants Cyn to have at any given moment, day, week, or month. The only way Cyn may have control of her own emotions and the room would be locked, prohibiting Red from entering it, was if she looked in the mirror and told her feelings to shut up. She would tell her emotions that she chose to let God take control, but when Cyn is in a vulnerable state, the door to her emotions flings open, giving Red access. The mood room not only controls Cyn's emotions, but it also controls her thoughts and words. Anytime Red saw that Cyn had given access to depression, he would invite a friend that had entered the house through a traumatic moment. For example, when Cyn lost her grandmother, Fellan entered the house and Red invited Fellan in the mood room to help him control her words and thoughts.

At one point, Red had passionately wanted someone out of the house after he found out that the person had been spreading toxic rumors around the house to get things out of control. This happened multiple times.

Everyone wants access to the mood room, but not as much as Jez. She is another generational issue like R.J., but she was kicked out of the house by Red after trying to gain access to the mood room. In other words, she'd tried to undermine and usurp Red's authority.

# THE JEZEBEL SPIRIT

*The spirit of Jezebel is a term used to describe a particular type of evil spirit that is mentioned in the Bible. This spirit is often associated with a woman named Jezebel who appears in the Old Testament as the wife of King Ahab of Israel. Jezebel was a pagan queen who worshiped false gods and was known for her wickedness and manipulative ways.*

*The spirit of Jezebel is characterized by a desire for power and control; it is a spirit of rebellion that rises against God and His authority, and it has a tendency to use manipulation and deception to achieve its goals. This spirit is often associated with sexual immorality, idolatry, and witchcraft.*

*In Revelation 2:20-23, Jesus speaks to the church in Thyatira and warns them about a woman who is called Jezebel. He says, "Nevertheless, I have this against you: You tolerate that woman Jezebel, who calls herself a prophet. By her teaching she misleads my servants into sexual immorality and the eating of food sacrificed to idols. I have given her time to repent of her immorality, but she is unwilling. So, I will cast her on a bed of suffering,* and I will make those who commit adultery with her suffer intensely, unless they repent of her ways. I will strike her children dead. Then all the churches will know that I am he who searches hearts and minds, and I will repay each of you according to your deeds."

This passage suggests that the spirit of Jezebel is a dangerous and destructive force that can infiltrate the church and lead believers astray. It is a spirit that seeks to destroy the work of God by promoting false teachings, seducing believers into sexual sin and other forms of immorality, and promoting the worship of false gods.

Breaking free from the spirit of Jezebel requires recognition of its presence and a commitment to turn away from its influence. It involves seeking God's truth and guidance, renouncing any ties to the spirit of rebellion, and submitting to God's authority in all areas of life. It also involves seeking accountability from other believers and being willing to confront and rebuke any manifestations of the spirit of Jezebel in our own lives or in the church.

## CHAPTER 5

# HELLO, JEZ

*(Three years ago...)*

Jez is short for Jezebel. The Jezebel spirit is very controlling, manipulative, and evil. The Jezebel spirit is always motivated by its own agenda, and it relentlessly pursues it. It's intentional about getting what it wants. There may be one in every family trying to govern, arrange, and fix everyone. In this case, there is one in every house.

KNOCK, KNOCK, KNOCK! A loud noise from the door startled Red while he was at his desk working. Red usually has an idea of who is at the door before they even knock, but for some reason, this visit took him by surprise.

"Who's there?!" yells Red from the desk he'd placed in his front room.

"Hello, I'm Jez," answers the person behind the door.

*Her voice is so captivating and lovely, almost as if she is singing as she speaks. It gives Red chills.*

Red ponders for a moment before he responds. "Who is this person?" Red thinks to himself. "Okay, come in!" Red finally responds.

The creaking sound of the door opening echoes throughout the house. As the tall, black wooden door opens, in steps a pale, yet beautiful,shaggy haired woman withjet-black hair and red lips that you could spot a mile away. Her trench coat is the color of the soft cream-colored carpet. Her hair flows with the breeze that comes in as she closes the door behind her.

"Oh, hello. I remember you. How have you been?" Red says with half a smile on his blushing, red freckled face.

Jez is a founding member of the house, but she always returns and she looks different every time. But this time is very different. Her voice sounds more mature and mellow toned.

Jez is known for betraying the ones that brought her to the house. The last person who brought her in before R.J. was Sal. During that time, Jez had long, curly black hair, plus, she was much bigger. Her skin was paler and she had braces. Her goal was to get everyone out of the house so she could take over. Red noticed her games so he decided to get Cyn to denounce her ways. Red made Cyn aware of the devious nature that was in her house by leading her to the closet to write in her journal at a young age. Whenever Red wanted someone out, he had a special way of doing so.

Jez wants Robin to find access to the mood room so Jez can be in control of everything and everyone. Jez has a way of manipulating and persuading individuals. Sometimes, all she has to do is look at someone long enough. It is very creepy.

It frustrated her that this never worked on Red. He'd figured her out early.

"Hi there. I knew you would remember me. I'm doing lovely. How are you, Mr. Red?" Jez responds.

Jez is not too fond of Red, but she will not let him know that.

*Before Red could respond to Jez's question, she cuts him off by asking where the restroom is located, even though she unmistakably knows where it is. She wants to get close to the mood room again.*

"Where is your restroom located?" asks Jez. "I don't recall where it is. It's been a while."

Red ignores Jez's question because he doesn't have time for her manipulative ways.
"Okay, I will just find my way then," Jez mumbles as she begins to scan the house.

Jez finds her way past the front room to the

hallway. She then walks past the mood room and stops to try and see what is going on in there. There is a red glow coming from underneath the door that draws Jez's attention.

*Jez looks to her left and gazes off into space while she is in the middle of the hallway. She begins to have a flashback of the moment when she was kicked out of the house the first time.*

"Jez!! How did you get in here?" Red screams with anger.
"It was open," Jez responds.

*Jez knows that she had manipulated a fellow residents to get Red to keep the door open so she could sneak into the room, but saying that the door is open still gave her a plausible excuse.*

*Red is highly upset to the point his face turns as red as his fiery red hair.*

*"GET OUT! You cannot be in here! Only I have*

the authority to be here! Matter of fact, *GET OUT THE HOUSE!"* Red screams at the top of his lungs.

*Red starts to throw things around the room. He picks up a lamp and throws it against the wall. The shattered glass splatters around the room, falling into the carpet. The base of the lamp hits the stern steel door before making a loud noise that resounds throughout the room.*

Jez is not bothered by the chaos that Red is creating. She stands there with her petite arms crossed while blowing on her nails as she waits for Red to calm down. She even keeps a smirk on her face as if she is amused by Red's anger.

"Are you done having a temper tantrum, sir?" asks Jez. Red ignores Jez as he has his back turned to her. He begins to write words on the wall to get Jez out of the house. He is so angry that Jez has gotten into the room, not only because she is in there without his permission, but because she tricked him into leaving the door open. When you leave the door open to the mood room, it gives room for anything and everything to enter and mess up the mood of Cyn. Red hates for everything to be out of his control, even for a second.

*Red continues to write words on the wall.*

He writes: anger, frustration, fed up! Get rid of manipulation, get rid of sneakiness, betrayal, etc.

Jez shakes her head and leaves the room. As she walks out of the room, she starts to head towards the door to exit the house, but she stops and pauses because she hears something.

"Jezebel, you foul, manipulative spirit, you no longer have access to this house! GET OUT!" Cynthia says.

*Cynthia is in her favorite closet praying and denouncing some things in her life. She is very young, yet, her denouncing doesn't sound like an adult breaking curses. Her denouncing sounds like a child telling her daddy to help her to be good and asking God to take away her evil ways. Little does she know that her words have power, even if they are controlled by her feelings.*

Some people leave while kicking and screaming, but Jez walks out calmly knowing that she will return. This is the first time Jez has left on her own, but it will not be the last. She has a record of coming in and out of people's lives. Jez continues to head towards the door. After passing the kitchen, she grabs her coat that is hanging by the door and slowly turns the knob to the front door.

"Goodbye, house! I will be back," she says as the wind from outside enters the house and blows the curtains that are on the window like a dramatic scene in a movie.

Red is still in the mood room changing things around. He removes the big red couch cover that is up against the wall to the left entering the room. He places a black cover over the couch and sits the lamp next to it. He then begins to get paint out of the small closet. He chooses green paint for the large windows. The windows are also an entrance into the room, but Red keeps it sealed tight so no one can come in without his notice. He spends all day in the room adding his touches to keep things in order after getting off track from when Jez entered. He wants it to look like a totally different room to anyone who would enter it next.

"Now that Jez is gone, it's time to go see what she put in the heads of my fellow friends who are also in the house," Red murmurs as he paints the window with the green paint. The paint begins to run down his hairy arm.

*Jez notices that she is standing in the middle of the hallway dozed off in a daydream.*

"Whew, okay! Let me head towards the restroom before Red thinks that I am up to no good again," Jez says to herself as she fixes the collar on her dress.

This is Jez's third return to the house, thus the reason she already has a bad relationship with Red. She doesn't want to get kicked out so early again. If she leaves, it will be on her terms.

Red is still sitting at his desk puzzled as to why Jez has returned to the house so soon. He never experienced the return of a resident so soon after being kicked out.

"Where did she go?" Red thinks to himself.

*Red is hoping she isn't trying to get in the mood room after only being there for a few minutes. He does not want to be the reason she leavesso soon again. He begins to work on Cyn's emotional records via his laptop and regains focus on what he was doing before Jez took him off track.*

Jez is in the restroom looking in the mirror at her flawless skin. While perfecting her makeup, she begins to think of a master plan. She is determined to take control of the house without Red figuring her out again. She opens the door to leave the restroom. The sound of the door reminds her of the time Cynthia was going into the stupid closet that everyone hates. Every time Cynthia goes into that closet with the old squeaky door, a cringe feeling overwhelms everyone in the house. Everyone starts to get nervous about who is leaving next. Jez walks out of the old-fashioned bathroom and looks at the door to the mood room. There is no glow coming from underneath the door anymore so she may not need to manipulate anyone to get in. Whenever the glow is gone, that means that the door is unlocked.

Jez walks up to the door with no fear at all and tries to turn the knob. The knob will not nudge, so she tries to push it open. The door opens, but it has so much weight to it that she has to put all of her weight into the push. Finally, the door opens just enough for her to squeeze in the space between the door and the wall. She gets in and takes a deep breath. This is one of the first times she gets nervous because it was too easy. The door suddenly shuts behind her and makes her flinch.

"Oh my!" Jez shouts as she places her hand on her chest. "Maybe, I should lock the door so no one else can enter," she reasons within herself.

So, she grabs the knob and begins to lock the door with her other hand.

"This was too easy," Jez exhales with a soft whisper.

Jez has finally gotten into the mood room, but little does she know, Red had previously installed a camera in the room since the last incident a few years ago. There are four cameras inside the room in each top corner of the walls.

Jez begins to look for the mysterious mood log computer that changes the system linked to the entire operation of the house. She stands right in the middle of the room and begins to search around it with a sparkle in her eyes. This logbook computer is so important that she can't miss this chance. She finally locates the computer over by the window; it was behind a weird-looking glass table that was camouflaged to blend in with the wall. She walks over to the window and grabs the small silver computer pad. She suddenly hears steps heading towards her, so she hurries and tries to erase Red's information. With her fingers typing away, she starts to type her name in the control system. Sweat is dripping down her face as it starts to get hot in the room.

Jez has changed the entire atmosphere of the room. That's when she hears the footsteps getting closer. She looks over by the window and finds the space to lay the logbook back in its rightful place.

Jez stands up from the black couch in the room and walks towards the steel door.

KNOCK KNOCK!

"Why is this door locked?" Red yells.

*Jez covers her mouth, looks around, and tries not to giggle. She is not intimidated by anyone in the house, including Red.*

Red continues to bang on the door while yelling out, "Jez, I know you are in there! Come out now! I have cameras! Unlock this door! What did you do?"

All of the commotion catches the attention of the others in the house. R.J., Sal, Robin, and Lacy all come running from the kitchen towards the mood room where Red is to see what was going on.

Curious and nervous, R.J. asks, "What's all the yelling for, bro?"

Red is so full of rage that he cannot hear anything but his own heavy breathing and knocking.

"Jez! GET OUT OF THERE! I'm breaking this door down in a second if you don't open it now!" Red shouts.

Jez is standing on the other side of the door

sneering and deciding how dramatic of an exit she should make after she opens the door. She grabs the handle of the door, and with all of her strength, she pulls the door open. Red and R.J. push the door open from the opposite side. Jez backs up as Red runs in the room and looks around to see what has been changed. He looks over by the window where the logbook tablet is to see if it has been tampered with. Jez walks around everyone standing at the door. She goes through the front room and opens the front door to exit. This time, she isn't necessarily kicked out; instead, she leaves the house before it happens.

# THE SPIRIT OF PERVERSION

*The spirit of perversion is a destructive force that can lead individuals and society as a whole away from God's intended purposes. Perversion is defined as the act of distorting something from its original purpose or natural state. In the Bible, perversion is often associated with sexual immorality, but it can also manifest in other areas of life, such as speech, behavior, and thought patterns.*

*In Deuteronomy 23:17, the Lord commanded His people, "There shall be no whore of the daughters of Israel, nor a sodomite of the sons of Israel." This verse makes it clear that sexual perversion is not part of God's plan for His people. In Romans 1:24-27, Paul describes the consequences of rejecting God and giving into sexual perversion, saying, "Therefore God also gave them up to uncleanness, in the lusts of their hearts, to dishonor their bodies among themselves, who exchanged the truth of God for the lie, and worshiped and served the creature rather than the Creator, who is blessed forever. Amen. For this reason God gave them up to vile passions. For even their women exchanged* the natural use for what is against nature. Likewise also the men, leaving the natural use of the woman, burned in their lust for one another, men with men committing what is shameful, and receiving in themselves the penalty of their error which was due."

The spirit of perversion can also manifest in other areas of life, such as speech and behavior. Proverbs 10:31-32 says, "The mouth of the righteous brings forth wisdom, but the perverse tongue will be cut out. The lips of the righteous know what is acceptable, but the mouth of the wicked speaks perverse things." This verse reminds us that the words we speak can be either righteous or perverse, and that our speech has the power to build up or tear down others.

Breaking free from the spirit of perversion requires a willingness to turn away from sinful thoughts and behaviors, and turn towards God's truth and righteousness. In 1 Corinthians 6:9-11, Paul tells the Corinthians, "Do not be deceived. Neither fornicators, nor idolaters, nor adulterers, nor homosexuals, nor sodomites, nor thieves, nor covetous, nor drunkards, nor revilers, nor extortioners will inherit the kingdom of God. And *such were some of you. But you were washed, but you were sanctified, but you were justified in the name of the Lord Jesus and by the Spirit of our God." This verse reminds us that no matter what sins we have committed, we can be washed clean and made new through the power of Jesus Christ.*

*. Sexual immorality, perverse speech and behavior, and distorted thought patterns are all signs of the spirit of perversion. Breaking free from this spirit requires a willingness to turn towards God's truth and righteousness and turn away from sinful thoughts and behaviors. By seeking God's truth and living in obedience to Him, we can break free from the spirit of perversion and live a life of freedom and purity.*

## CHAPTER 6

# BACK TO REALITY, PERVERTED PETE

The Copeland's are getting ready to go on their summer vacation. Every summer, Ruth takes the kids on a fun trip. This particular year, there is a guest coming along.

"Mommy!" the seven-year-old girl yells.
"Yes, Bookie," Ruth replies.
"Does Daddy have to come with us to Florida?" Cynthia whines.

*Ruth gives her daughter a puzzled look; she then turns around to talk to Cynthia as she bends down to look her in the eyes.*

Ruth responds, "You don't want your daddy coming along with us? I thought you wanted him to come so you could get to know him more. This was your brother's idea, not mine."

"No! Daddy isn't my favorite! I want it to be us three just like it used to be," Cynthia yells as she runs away to her favorite closet.

Ruth is surprised to witness such a dramatic reaction from Cynthia. Cynthia has never acted this way towards her father. This is very strange. Concerned, Ruth walks out of the kitchen and heads down the hallway towards her son's room. Andre is 12-years old now. He is playing his video game as always when his mother enters the room. Ruth knocks on the door and softly says, "Baby, are you sleeping?"

Andre answers, "No, Ma. What's up? Come in."
"I know I can come in; this is my house," Ruth jokingly responds.

*Andre does not pay his mother any attention. He is focused on the game he is currently losing.*

"Yes, Ma. What's up? Are you ready to go yet?" Andre asks.
"In a few, baby. Do you know what's going on

with your sister?" Ruth asks.

*Andre is reacting to the game he is playing.*

"AHHH man, I lost! Oh, what you say about Cyn, Ma?" Andre responds.
"Yea, she is acting weird about your father coming with us to Florida. You know I don't like him, but I thought it would make you guys happy," Ruth says.
"Man, you know how she is, Ma. I think it's her hormones or something. You know she is about to turn eight, so doesn't her girl stuff start making her act weird?" Andre asks.

*Ruth rolls her eyes and smacks her teeth. She doesn't know why she even asked Andre because all he cares about is his silly games.*

Ruth lets out a big sigh and throws her hands in the air, waving away Andre."Uggh! Whatever, Dre. Come and put your shoes on and get off that stupid game," Ruth says as she smacks her teeth and walks out of her son's room. She walks across the hall to her room to get her things, along with her cell phone so she can call Frank and get his location.

Cynthia is in the closet hosting a bad attitude while sitting on the dark red carpet. She doesn't want her Daddy to come on vacation with them, so she prays to God about it. She reasons within herself that He is the only one who can help her; He is the only one she can talk to about her secret.

"Daddy, you are my real Daddy. That other man is a meany and I am scared of him. Can you please help me? If we go on vacation together, he is going to touch me in places I don't like and make me very scared. I don't want to tell Mommy or Dre because they will not believe me. No one believes me. But I know you believe me, God. I know you love me. Maybe, you can't help me because you are in the sky so you won't get to me in time. My Mommy told me that you can be in many places at one time. So, can you come down if he touches me this time? Thank you, God. AMEN!" Cynthia prays.

Cynthia stands to her tiny feet as she opens the door to the closet. When she opens the door, she sees her mother sitting in the den on the chocolate brown couch staring at her with an angry face and tears welling up in her eyes.

"Oh my God," Ruth shakes her head and whispers as tears stream down her face.

Cynthia runs up to Ruth and asks, "What's wrong, Mommy? Why are you crying?"

*As the little curly-headed girl questions her mother, her voice begins to crack because she doesn't like to see her mommy crying. Cynthia likes everyone to be happy, even if it means she has to suffer.*

Ruth grasps Cynthia in her arms and places her head on Cynthia's chest.

"I'm so sorry, Bookie! I didn't know he was touching you. Why didn't you tell me?" Ruth cries. "I'm sorry, Mommy! I'm so sorry!" Cynthia sobs.

"No, baby, I'm sorry Mommy didn't protect you," Ruth says to her innocent daughter.

Ruth feels horrible because she knows exactly how it feels to be touched inappropriately by her father and even other family members. She'd made a promise to herself that she would protect her child one day from all the monsters that would attempt to steal a child's innocence.

*Ruth grabs Cynthia's face and looks her straight in the eyes before saying with her lips balled up,* "I promise you, Bookie, he will NEVER; I mean it, Bookie—NEVER EVER touch you again."

Cynthia starts to cry harder because she has always wanted to feel protected by her mommy or by anyone, for that matter. She can't believe her mommy was listening to her prayer. What else did Ruth hear that Cynthia may not know of? This is the first time Cynthia and Ruth has bonded since she was an infant.

## Chapter 6: Back to Reality, Perverted Pete

*Suddenly, their doorbell rings and Dre runs from the back room to the front door with excitement!*

"DAD!" the twelve-year old screams with so much joy.

Andre places his hand on the gold door handle of the screen glass door. He pulls the door open and jumps into the arms of his tall, dark-skinned father.

"What's up, lil Dre boy?" Frank responds as he smiles with his gold tooth glistening.
"Dad, I am so happy you are coming with us to Disney Land!" Andre says.

Little do the guys know that there is another completely opposite set of emotions sitting in the room next to them. Cynthia and Ruth are still in the den talking about how Cynthia is terrified of her father.

"Where are the girls?" Frank asks Andre.

"They are in the den," Andre responds.

Frank puts Andre down and walks past the

living room couch. The vintage furniture reminds him of his mother's house. He walks out of the living room and looks into the kitchen. Frank used to live in the Copeland household when he and Ruth were married, so walking through the house brings back loving memories.

Frank finally walks to the den and notices Ruth with Cynthia lying in her mother's arms.
"Hey, my baby!" Frank says to Cynthia with a big and warming smile.

Cynthia jumps out of her mother's arms, runs from the couch to the closet door. She then opens it to get inside and hide from Frank. Ruth gets up calmly from the couch and walks right past Frank to get to the hallway. As she walks past Frank, her shoulder brushes against his muscular bare arms. She walks down the hallway towards her bedroom and shuts the door behind her. Frank is standing in the room with a puzzled look on his face. He walks up to the wooden brown door of the closet and whispers to Cynthia.

"Come out, baby, and give Daddy a hug. I

haven't seen you in a long time."
"NO! GO AWAY!" screams Cynthia.

Frank feels something against the back of his neck. He then hears something click.
*Ruth whispers in a strong, passionate, and deep voice while standing behind Frank with a black 9-millimeter Glock pointed at the back of his neck. She loads the chamber and says,*
"Don't you ever touch or place a finger on my child again."

"What are you doing, Ruth? What is wrong with you? Put the gun down, girl. Cynthia is my child too," Frank says as he places his hands up in surrender.
"Get out of my house before I do something I will not regret doing," Ruth angrily whispers.

"MOMMY! WHAT ARE YOU DOING TO DADDY?" Andre cries out.
"Babe, go to your room and close the door," Ruth tells Andre.
"But MOMMY! Why are you doing this?" Andre whines.
"GO! NOW!" Ruth yells.

Andre runs to the back. He thumps each step on the ground with his feet to release his emotions.

*In the closet is a frightened Cynthia crying her heart out. She doesn't know what to do but hide in the place where she feels protected from her family.*

"Ruth, calm down! What's going on? Let's sit down and talk!" Frank dramatically yells.
"NO! There is no talking needed! Get the hell out of my house before I put a bullet in the back of your head," Ruth cries.
"Ruth! Please, calm down!" Frank yells.

Frank turns around slowly and looks Ruth in her eyes. He can see the hatred and anger. He grabs the gun and places it on the floor next to his feet. He lifts his hands and places them on Ruth's shoulder. Ruth grabs his arms and removes them from her.

"Get your filthy hands off of me! Get out of my house, Frank!" Ruth yells.

Ruth slaps Frank in the face and pushes him to the floor. Franks places his hand on his face and looks up at Ruth from the floor. He has a confused and yet angry expression on his face.

The closet door squeals as it opens. Cynthia crawls out of the closet. The door hits the gun that is lying on the carpet. Cynthia then grabs the gun and holds it up in the air.

"Cynthia!" Frank and Ruth yell in unison.

Cynthia interrupts the two of them and places her little fingers on the trigger as it shoots up to the ceiling.

"Get out, Daddy!" yells Cynthia.

Ruth reaches out to grab Cynthia. She then picks her up, carries her on her hip, and walks out of the room towards the hallway.

"Bookie, are you okay!" Ruth asks.
"Mommy, can we go! Am I in trouble?" Cynthia cries out.

"No, baby. You're not in any trouble. Come on. Let's go check on your brother," Ruth says. Frank is still on the floor in the room. He is in shock and confusion. He finally finds the energy to get up and sit on the couch. He rubs his head and looks up at the bullet hole in the ceiling.

Ruth and Cynthia walk down the small hallway towards Andre's door. Ruth grabs the doorknob with her left hand and turns it. When she opens the door and skims the room with her small brown eyes, she notices that Andre is nowhere to be found. Andre hides all the time when he is upset or scared. Ruth gently places Cynthia down on the floor so she can start to look around the room for Andre.

"Dre! Stop hiding and come out here. We have to go!" Ruth yells.

Andre does not respond. Ruth starts to search around the room. She walks to his bed and looks under it, but she doesn't see him. She then walks to his walk-in closet. She opens the door and hopes to see him hiding behind the clothes that are piled up on the carpet. She feels a breeze come in the room. It blows the flowy, bright green blouse she's wearing. Ruth turns around and notices that the window is open. She walks up to the window and sticks her head out to see if Andre is outside sitting on the front porch. The window is not too far from the ground, so it doesn't take much to climb out of it.

"Mommy, where did Dre go?" Cynthia asks. "He is probably just hiding somewhere outside, Bookie. Don't worry. I will go get him," Ruth responds in a hushed tone.

Ruth did not want to seem worried in front of Cynthia, and she surely did not want to tell that monster of a father what had just taken place. Ruth walks out of Andre's room and heads towards the den to tell Frank to leave. As she walks down the hall, Cynthia follows her and hugs her mother's hips.

"Mommy, can we go find Dre, please?" Cynthia

asks. Ruth looks down at Cynthia's little sweet face and responds, "Yes, give me a minute, Bookie. Go sit in my room until I come back."

"Okay," Cynthia says with disappointment in her tone.

Ruth walks in the den and stares into Frank's dark brown eyes. He has a bump on his head from the impact of her hitting him, but she is so furious that she simply does not care. All she wants is for him to be out of her house and out of their lives. Ruth is crazy enough to kill him, but she has two kids to worry about. She doesn't want to abandon them by going to jail.

"Frank, didn't I tell you to leave? I will call the police if I have to," Ruth says.

Frank is still acting as if Ruth has lost her mind. He is too prideful to admit ever touching his little girl inappropriately. He is, in fact, too embarrassed to look Cynthia in the face after Ruth found out. Frank finally gives in and stands up from the couch.

"No, we don't need to scare the kids anymore than we already have. I'll just leave. Tell the kids I love them and I'm sorry," Frank says as he walks out of the room and towards the front door.

He slowly paces his way to the door. As he opens the glass screen, he notices Andre sitting on the steps.

"Lil Man, what are you doing out here?" Frank asks Andre.
"Dad, I want you to come with us. I don't know what is going on, but I just want us to be a big happy family again," Andre whines.

Frank feels so badly for all the commotion that has just taken place that he is not prepared to have a heart-to-heart conversation with his twelve-year old son. He walks towards the brick steps and sits beside Andre. Andre does not look too happy, so Frank knows that this is not a good time to explain anything.

"Man, don't worry about anything right now. Dre, just go have fun with your mother and sister. Remember, you have to be the man of the house. I'll see you when you come back," says Frank.

Andre looks up at his Dad's face and he somehow knows that he isn't going to see him again for a long time. He is used to his Dad lying to him, so the lies do not bother him as much as they once did.

"Okay, Dad," Andre sighs.
"Alright, son. Go ahead in the house and check on your girls. I'm out," Frank responds.

Frank gets up and wipes the dirt off of his gray jeans. He then begins to walk towards the gate that surrounds the house. Andre watches Frank as he walks away like he always does, never really returning for years on end. He knows this may be the last time for a while that he sees his Dad.

Andre gets up from the porch and walks up the

steps to enter the house. He opens the screen door and sees Ruth sitting on the living room chair.

"I don't want to talk about it," Andre mumbles as he walks through the front room.

"Well, I don't care what you don't want to talk about. I want to know why you climbed out the window like a thief," Ruth says sarcastically.

"Ma, can we just go and forget all of this ever happened?" whines Andre.

"Boy, stop whining and come here. Look at me when you speak to me," Ruth yells.

Andre turns around and looks at his mother with tears streaming down his face. He walks to the fancy floral chair and plops down with his arms folded.

"Okay, Ma," responds Andre.

Ruth and Andre have a mother-and-son moment while little Cynthia is still in her mother's room waiting for them to go on their summer vacation. Even after the Mommy and daughter moment they'd experienced minutes ago, Cynthia still feels like things should be about her in that moment, and not about her brother. It is very rare that she receives warmhearted attention from her mother. Andre's moment with his mother causes Cynthia to feel rejected, as usual. After all, her mother has just found out that Cynthia had been molested by her father, so in this very moment, Cynthia feels alone and overlooked.

# THE SPIRIT OF DEPRESSION

*Depression is a condition that affects millions of people around the world. It is characterized by feelings of sadness, hopelessness, and despair that can last for weeks, months, or even years. From a biblical perspective, depression is often associated with a spiritual battle, as the enemy seeks to rob individuals of their joy and hope in God.*

*The Bible has many examples of people who experienced depression and struggled with feelings of despair. In Psalm 42:5, the psalmist cries out, "Why, my soul, are you downcast? Why so disturbed within me? Put your hope in God, for I will yet praise him, my Savior and my God." This verse reminds us that even those who are faithful to God can experience feelings of despair and depression.*

*In 1 Kings 19, we see the prophet Elijah experiencing depression after a great victory over the prophets of Baal. Despite his success, he became fearful and ran away from Jezebel, eventually ending up in a cave where he cried out to God. In his despair, he asked God to take his life,* but instead, God provided for him and encouraged him to continue in his calling.

The spirit of depression can also be caused by a number of physical, emotional, and spiritual factors. It may be the result of a chemical imbalance in the brain, a traumatic event, or unresolved emotional pain. However, it is important to recognize that depression can also be a spiritual battle. In Ephesians 6:12, Paul tells us, "For our struggle is not against flesh and blood, but against the rulers, against the authorities, against the powers of this dark world and against the spiritual forces of evil in the heavenly realms."

Breaking free from the spirit of depression requires a holistic approach that addresses the physical, emotional, and spiritual aspects of the condition. This may involve seeking medical treatment, counseling, and support from friends and family. It also involves turning towards God and seeking His truth and guidance in the midst of the struggle. In Psalm 34:17-18, the psalmist writes, "The righteous cry out, and the Lord hears them; he delivers them from all their troubles. The Lord is close to the brokenhearted and saves those who are crushed in spirit."

*Breaking free from this spirit requires a holistic approach that addresses the physical, emotional, and spiritual aspects of the condition. By seeking God's truth and guidance and relying on His strength and provision, individuals can find hope and healing in the midst of depression.*

# CHAPTER 7

## SAL

*Most of the time, the thought of a thing will give an unwanted person access back into the house. Perversion came in when Cynthia started getting molested by her father. Even though it was not her fault, it became her fight. After being invaded mentally and physically, Cynthia's house had been invaded spiritually. Some traumatic events may cause a lifetime of mental issues. Pete is an issue that came without Cynthia opening the door.*

Cynthia had a moment where perversion may have left her life, but once her Dad came back, it brought back memories that gave Pete access back into the house. Sometimes, it only takes a memory, and boom, it's back. The memory will ignite a feeling, and if you are not strong enough to resist the thoughts, those feelings will take control and influence your decisions. The decision can be just a phone call that ignites a trigger once the phone is answered. Now perversion has been given an opportunity.

This time, he forces his way in, instead of knocking. Pete is an unpleasant character that everyone in the house is annoyed with except for two individuals. Lacy is his daughter and Sal is his best friend in the house.

The sound of the front door getting kicked down alerts everyone in the kitchen. Red is in the back lying down sleeping, which he doesn't do too much, but the Charlotte issue has worn him out.

The door falls off its hinges and hits the floor, making an alarming sound. R.J., Sal, Charlotte, and Lacy all run from the kitchen to the front room to see what has happened.

"Hello, everyone! I'm back like I never left!" Pete yells as he steps inside the house after kicking the door down.

"Pete, why did you have to kick down the door?" R.J. asks.

*Pete's presence and his dramatic entrance annoys R.J.*

"Because I like to make a scene whenever I am entering," Pete responds.

R.J. smacks his teeth and turns around to head back to the kitchen. When he turns around, he notices the mood room's door is open and Red is nowhere to be found. Nevertheless, he shrugs his shoulders and keeps moving towards the kitchen to finish eating his breakfast.

The rest of the crew is still in the front talking to Pete. Lacy and Sal are so happy to see Pete, but Charlotte does not care as much to see him.

"Hi, Dad." Lacy says.
"Hey, sweet thang! How are you?" Pete asks while walking up to his daughter and reaching

out his arms to hug her.

"I'm great, Dad. It's pretty boring here. How did you come back?" Lacy asks inquisitively.

Pete, while hugging her, looks into his daughter's green eyes and says, "Frank returned home so I found my way in!"

"Oh, okay" Lacy responds.

Lacy walks away from her father and heads back to the kitchen where R.J., Robin and Hannah are. She is confused about who Frank is so she just smiles at Pete and starts thinking about how hungry she is as she rubs her stomach.

Frank has always brought perversion into Cynthia's life. His abusive ways give her unwanted thoughts and nightmares. These thoughts and nightmares are points of access; they allow Pete to enter into the house all over again. It doesn't take much to give a spirit access, especially as a child. When their eyes are opened up as a result of molestation, perversion creeps in like a snake. Pete is very sneaky. Sal and Pete are best friends because he is very sneaky as well.

Sal is ecstatic to see his best friend, so he walks up to him and slaps Pete on his back.

"What's up, old man?" Sal shouts.
"Old man?! Man, please. I am still young and kicking it," Pete responds.
"The fact that you just said kicking it proves that you are old, my friend," Sal answers.

Sal and Pete are like Frick and Frack. They cannot be separated once together. Pete is back so Sal now has a partner in crime. They can now continue their twisted jokes and crazy games.

"Where's Mr. CEO himself?" Pete asks Sal.
"Who?" Sal responds.
"Red, man!" Pete yells.
"Oh, he is in the back asleep," says Sal.
"Sleep? When did he start doing that?" Pete says as he erupts with laughter.
"Ha, man, one needs to sleep," Sal answers.

Sal and Pete continue their conversation while trying to put the door back on its hinges before Red sees it and throws a fit. As the two silly guys put up the door, they hear footsteps coming from the hallway. The footsteps are getting closer and closer, and then they suddenly stop.

"Hi there, fellas," Jez softly speaks.

Pete and Sal are standing beside each other with their eyes as wide as two owls. Pete squeezes Sal's hand with nervousness.

*Jez and Sal have had issues in the past. She has and will always have Sal wrapped around her fingers. Yes, multiple of them!*

"Are you fellas okay?" asks Jez as she twirls her blonde curls with her index finger.
"So, where did you come from, Jez?" Pete asks.
"Are you okay, man?" Sal whispers to Pete.
"Yes, I am more concerned for you! Aren't you nervous to see her?" Pete responds.
Sal answers, "You know I have to play it cool. I

don't want her to see me sweat."
"We can all see that you are sweating, Sal,"
Pete says calmly.

*Jez and Sal have a lot of unfinished business.
This is what brings the proverbial "elephant in
the room" when they are around one another.
The two ex-rivals are not going to break the
awkwardness because they are too prideful to
share their emotions. Jez will never let a single
soul see her emotions. It's as if she does not
have a heart.*

Jez can tell that Pete and Sal are whispering
about her, so she approaches them. "What are
you two talking about?" Jez asks with a sly
smile on her face.

Pete and Sal are taken aback by Jez's sudden
appearance, but they try to remain calm. "We
were just talking about how we could help
you," Pete says, trying to diffuse the situation.

But Jez isn't fooled by their words. She knows
that Pete and Sal are her rivals and that they do
not like her. "You don't need to help me," Jez

replies. "I can take care of myself. And as for you two, you should be careful. I know what you're up to, and I won't let you get in my way."

Pete and Sal are shocked by Jez's bold words, but they don't know what to do. They realize that Jez is a Jezebel spirit, known for her manipulative ways and deceptive practices. They know that they have to be careful around her and not let her influence the other spirits that are in the house.

From that day on, Pete and Sal keep a close eye on Jez, making sure that she doesn't cause any more trouble in the house.

# CHAPTER 8

## SAL MEETS JEZ

Sal is a spirit unlike any other spirit in the house. He is unique in his nature. He has a powerful presence that can be felt by anyone nearby. His only goal in life is to bring depression into the lives of anyone connected to him.

Sal has been around for centuries, but he has never found anyone who was truly susceptible to his personality. That is, until he met Cyn. Because of Jez, Cyn has been struggling with anxiety and low self-esteem for years. She is the perfect target for Sal's dark thoughts.

Sal begins to visit Cyn in her dreams. At first, he simply whispers negative thoughts into her ear, telling her that she isn't good enough, that she is a burden on those around her, and that she will never be happy. But as time goes on, Sal's influence grows stronger, and he is able to manifest himself in the physical world—something that a lot of the others cannot do.

*The spirit of depression has its way of entering into someone's life by manifesting itself in so many colorful ways.*

*The Bible does not explicitly use the term "spirit of depression," but it does speak to the emotional struggles that can accompany depression. In Psalm 42:5, the psalmist cries out, "Why, my soul, are you downcast? Why so disturbed within me? Put your hope in God, for I will yet praise him, my Savior and my God." This verse acknowledges the heaviness of heart that can come with depression, but also offers a reminder to turn to God for hope and salvation. In Isaiah 61:3, the prophet writes that God will provide "a garment of praise instead of a spirit of despair (heaviness)." This verse suggests that God can replace the feelings of despair with a sense of joy and hope, bringing*

*comfort and healing to those struggling with
depression or struggling with Sal.*

Sal often appears to Cyn as a shadowy figure,
always lurking just out of sight. He whispers
horrible things to her, telling her that she is
worthless and that nobody cares about her.
Cyn tries to ignore him, but Sal's words have
begun to wear her down. She starts to believe
that he is right, and that she will never be
happy.

As Cyn sinks deeper into depression, Sal's
influence grows stronger. He is able to
manipulate her thoughts and feelings, making
it seem like there is no way out of the despair
she is in. Cyn feels like she is trapped in a
never-ending cycle of sadness and
hopelessness.

But one day, something changes. Cyn realizes
that Sal is not a force of nature, but a being
with its own agenda. She begins to fight back
against his influence, using positive
affirmations and therapy to combat the

negative thoughts he regularly plants in her mind.

Over time, Cyn is able to push Sal out of her life completely. She learns to love herself and to see the good in the world around her. Sal is left homeless, and he eventually fades away with nowhere to go and no place to land. That was until Jez came to the rescue.

Jez has always been a master-manipulator. With her striking blonde hair and piercing blue eyes, she has a way of getting what she wants from anyone she encounters. It is a skill that has served her well, allowing her to climb the ranks of the spirit world. But even Jez has her limits, and when she stumbles upon a depressive spirit named Sal, she knows that she has met her match.

Sal had been defeated, or so he thought. He has spent years tormenting a young girl named Cyn, feeding off her sadness and despair, but when Cyn finally found the strength to fight back and banish him from her life, Sal had been left adrift and alone. That is until Jez found him.

Jez has always been interested in bringing a force with her wherever she trampled, and when she stumbled upon Sal, she saw an opportunity to put her skills to the test. She knew she could use Sal to her advantage, and so, she went about bringing him back to the house.

*Red does not like Jez or Sal. They are a force when they are together. He cannot control them like he can control everyone else.*

It wasn't an easy task, but Jez is nothing if not persistent. She spent weeks studying the ancient texts and practicing the rituals needed to summon Sal's spirit back from the depths of defeat. And when she finally succeeded, she was overjoyed.

She wasted no time in putting Sal to work, sending him back into Cyn's life to wreak havoc once again. At first, Sal was hesitant. He knew what he had done to Cyn before, and he didn't want to go down that path again. But Jez was relentless, and she promised him power and glory if he would just do as she asked.

And so Sal fell back into old habits, tormenting Cyn with dark thoughts and feelings. It isn't long before Cyn is once again consumed by a deep and pervasive sadness, and Jez revels in her success. But as time goes on, Jez begins to realize that she has made a terrible mistake. She has unleashed a monster that she can no longer control, and Sal is stronger than she has ever imagined. She tries to banish him once again, but it is too late. Sal has grown too powerful, and he is no longer content with just tormenting Cyn. He wants more.

Jez watches in horror as Sal begins to consume everything in his path, leaving a trail of sadness and despair behind him. And as she witnesses the devastation he's wrought, she knows that she has made a terrible mistake.

Jez paces back and forth in the dark, damp cave where Sal loves to hang out. She is furious with him, and she doesn't care who knows it.

"You've gone too far, Sal," she snarls. "I thought you could handle this, but you've let things get out of control. You're bringing too much sorrow into Cyn's life."

Sal laughs, his eyes gleaming with a dark energy. "You knew what you were getting into when you brought me back," Sal retorts. "I warned you that I would not be contained. You thought you could control me, but you were wrong."

Jez feels a cold sweat break out on her forehead. She had no clue that Sal was going to take over her plans. She has made the mistake of bringing him back, and now she is paying the price for underestimating Sal. He is now a pest who keeps getting in the way of her strategies.

"You need to stop," Jez says, her voice quivering. "Cyn is mine. We are not a team!" Sal shrugs. "What does it matter?" he says. "She's just one person. There are millions of others we can torment. Why should we care about her?"

Jez feels a surge of anger rise up within her. "You're sick," she spits. "You're just like all the other demons I've dealt with over the years. You think you're above everyone else, but you're just a little pest!"

Sal's eyes narrow, and Jez can feel his anger building. "Watch your tongue, Jez," he growls. "I am not like the others. I am more powerful than you can imagine."

Jez knows that he is right. Sal is not like any other demon she has ever encountered. His powers are foreign; his will is more unyielding. She has made a mistake in thinking she could control him.

As they argue, Jez can feel the weight of Sal's influence growing stronger. She can sense the other spirits he brought with him, their dark energy filling the cave like a thick fog. She knows that they are causing even more sorrow and pain in Cyn's life.

"We need to stop this," she says, her voice shaking. "We need to end this now before it's too late."
Sal laughs again, releasing a cold, sinister sound. "It's already too late," he says. "We've already won. And there's nothing you can do to stop us."

*Jez is a mischievous spirit, known for her playful, yet manipulative antics among the other spirits. But when she'd heard about Cyn's encounter with Sal, a spirit known for bringing on depression and despair, she knew she had to act. Jez ponders for hours, searching for a way to lift Cyn's spirits and free her from Sal's grip. She knows that Cyn is strong, but she also knows that even the strongest can falter in the face of avid darkness. Finally, Jez has an idea. She decides to gather a group of like-minded spirits and create a powerful shield of positive energy around Cyn, one that would repel any negative influence that Sal may try to send her way. With this plan in place, Jez sets out to gather her allies and put her plan into action.*

*Sal thinks that he has won after their verbal altercation is over. Time passes, and he has not seen Jez in the house for a while. All he knows is that he has managed to gain control for now. Cyn does not know how to shake this depression.*

# CHAPTER 9

## FRANK OR PETE

Cynthia, or Cyn, as her friends call her, has been looking forward to her 16th birthday for months. She has planned every detail of her party, from the decorations to the music; she did this to ensure that it would be a night to remember. Ruth helped her with the preparations and Andre promised to DJ the event.

Cyn wakes up early on her birthday filled with excitement and anticipation. She spends the day getting ready, picking out the perfect outfit, and doing her hair and makeup. When her friends arrive for the party, they are greeted by a festive atmosphere filled with balloons, streamers, and twinkling lights. The music is pumping, and everyone is dancing and having a great time.

But then, in the middle of the party, Cyn's worst nightmare happens. Her father, Frank, arrives. Frank has not been a part of her life since she was seven-years old when he'd been confronted by her mother for molesting her. Cyn has mixed feelings about her father. On one hand, she has always wanted to have a relationship with him, but on the other hand, she struggles with feelings of anger and resentment towards him for leaving their family, along with so many other traumatic events that have haunted her for years.

When Frank walks into the room, Cyn's energy immediately shifts. She feels a knot form in her stomach as she watches him approach her. He looks different than she remembers; he's older and more tired-looking. He hugs her tightly, but Cyn feels stiff in his embrace. She tries to shake off her discomfort and introduce him to her friends, but the awkwardness lingers.

As the party continues, Cyn finds herself distracted and unable to fully enjoy herself. She can feel Frank's presence in the room, and it makes her anxious. At one point, she had even caught him talking to Ruth in a corner, and she couldn't help but overhear their conversation. They were arguing about money, and Cyn felt a wave of sadness wash over her.

Ruth and Frank's conversation grow more heated as they argue about money. They are in the kitchen, just out of the earshot of the party guests, but Cyn can hear every word from where she stands in the living room. At first, she tries to focus on the music and dance with her friends, but as the argument escalates, it becomes impossible to ignore.

"I can't believe you're asking me for more money," Ruth says, her voice shaking with anger. "I've been doing everything on my own for years now. You can't just swoop in and demand more from me."
"I'm not asking for more than I'm entitled to," Frank shoots back.
"I'm your children's father. I have a right to be a part of their lives and to support them financially."

*Cyn feels a pang of sadness as she listens to her parents argue. She hates that they are still fighting about the same things years after their divorce. She wishes they could just get along for her and Andre's sake.*

"I know that," Ruth says, her tone softening slightly."But you can't just expect me to hand over more money without any warning. I have bills to pay too, you know."

"I'm not trying to take advantage of you," Frank says, his voice calmer now. "But I'm struggling too. I've been out of work for months. I've got bills piling up just like you do."

*Cyn feels a surge of anger at her father's words. He has never been there for them, never contributed to their lives. He always comes in and creates traumatic events. He'd even taken advantage of Cyn, his own daughter, and now, he expects her mother to do any and everything for him. He was trying to guilt-trip her mother into giving him more money.*

"You should have thought about that before you left us," Ruth says, her voice filled with bitterness. "You can't just come back into our lives and expect everything to be the same. You have to earn back our trust and our respect. And that starts with being honest with us about your finances."

Cyn feels a flicker of hope as she listens to her mother's words. Maybe there is a chance for her family to heal and move forward together, but as she watches Frank storm out of the kitchen, she can't shake off the feeling that things are still far from resolved.

She hates that her family is still struggling with the same issues that tore them apart years ago.

Eventually, Frank leaves the party and Cyn tries to shake off the negative energy that he brought with him. She dances with her friends and blows out the candles on her cake, but the joy she had felt earlier in the night is gone. As her friends begin to leave, Cyn feels a sense of relief. She is ready for the night to be over.

As she climbs into bed that night, Cyn thinks about her birthday and how it went. She was unable to fully enjoy the celebration that she had worked so hard to plan. She can't shake off the feeling that something is wrong, that her family is still broken, and that her father's presence has only made things worse.

The next day, Cyn overhears her mother, Ruth, on the phone, speaking with Frank about a potential move.

"I can't keep living like this," Ruth says, her voice strained. "I need to do what's best for the kids. Maybe it's time for us to move away, start fresh somewhere else."

Cyn's heart sinks as she listens to the conversation. She can't imagine leaving her friends and everything she has ever known behind. And the thought of starting over in a new place with a family still in turmoil seems almost unbearable.

For the next few days, Cyn is consumed by thoughts of the potential move. She tries to talk to her mother about it, but Ruth is distant and preoccupied. Cyn feels alone and unsure of what to do. It isn't until she speaks with her brother, Andre, that Cyn begins to feel a sense of hope.

"We'll get through this," he tells her, placing a reassuring hand on her shoulder.
"We've been through worse before. And who knows? Maybe a change of scenery will be good for us."

Cyn thinks about Andre's words and begins to feel a sense of possibility. Maybe a move wouldn't be so bad after all. Maybe it would be a chance for her family to start over, heal old wounds, and build a new life together.

As the weeks go by, Cyn watches as her family makes plans for the move. They start packing up their belongings and saying goodbye to friends. Cyn feels a mix of sadness and excitement as she looks toward the future.

On the day of the move, Cyn looks around her

empty room and feels a sense of nostalgia wash over her. But as she walks out of the house with her family by her side, she feels a renewed sense of hope. She is ready for whatever lies ahead.

---

# CHAPTER 10

## REUNITED

*According to the Bible, the real world and the spiritual world are two distinct and separate realms. The real world, also known as the physical world, is the realm that we can perceive with our senses through touch, sight, taste, smell, and hearing. It is the world that we see around us, the one that we can touch and interact with.*

*On the other hand, the spiritual world is the realm that is beyond our physical senses. It is a realm that is inhabited by spiritual beings such as angels and demons, as well as God and other divine entities. This realm is not visible to us in the same way that the physical world is, but it is no less real.*
*The Bible teaches that the spiritual world is the ultimate reality from which the physical world derives its existence. In other words, the physical world is a reflection or manifestation of the spiritual world. The Bible also teaches that the spiritual*

*world is eternal, while the physical world is temporal, and will eventually pass away. Furthermore, the Bible teaches that the spiritual world has a significant impact on the physical world. For instance, it teaches that our actions in the physical world can have spiritual consequences, and that spiritual forces can influence events in the physical world. In other words, Cynthia is the house. Who, or shall I say what lives in your house?*

*Pete and Sal stop whispering and start to address Jez as she comes closer. The dialogue went this way:*

Pete: Hey Sal, I didn't know you knew Jez. What brings you back, Jez?

Jez: Hi Pete, good to see you again. I'm here to talk to Sal, and he should know why.

Sal: *(playing it cool)* Hey Jez, what's up?

Jez: *(addressing Sal directly)* Sal, I heard you've been spreading rumors about me. I don't appreciate that.

Sal: *(taken aback)* What? No, I haven't said anything about you.

Jez: *(firmly)* Don't lie to me, Sal. I have evidence that you've been talking behind my back.

Sal: *(defensive)* Look, Jez, I don't know what you're talking about. I haven't said anything bad about you.

Pete: *(trying to diffuse the tension)* Hey guys, let's calm down. Maybe this is just a misunderstanding.

Jez: *(ignoring Pete)* Sal, I don't have time for games *(smirks)*. If you have a problem with me, let's talk about it.

Sal: *(getting frustrated)* I don't have a problem with you, Jez. I barely even know you.

Jez: *(skeptical)* Then why...

Sal: *(defeated; cuts off Jez)* I don't know. Maybe someone's trying to stir up trouble.

Pete: *(trying to lighten the mood)* Well, let's not let this ruin our day. How about we grab some lunch in the kitchen and talk it out?

Jez: *(smiling)* That sounds like a good idea. I'm willing to let bygones be bygones if you are, Sal.

Sal: *(reluctantly)* Yeah, sure. Let's go get some food.

Pete: *(relieved)* Great, let's go then.

The new trio decides to head into the kitchen. Pete walks towards the stove to make his plate. Sal sneakily pulls Jez aside to air his concerns.

Sal: Jez, I need to talk to you. Now!

The blonde haired, blue eyed beauty rolls her eyes and thinks to herself, "Here he goes thinking he controls me."

Jez: What's the matter, Sal? *(As she places her hand on his shoulder).*

Sal: Don't touch me! I'm sick and tired of your little games with Cyn. You're just trying to get rid of me, aren't you?

Jez: *(smirking)* Of course not, Sal. I just think it's time for Cyn to move on from you.

Sal: You're just jealous because I have a stronger hold on her than you ever did.

Jez: Excuse me? I am more powerful than you can ever hope to be.

Sal: Ha! You may be more powerful, but you're nothing compared to my influence over Cyn.

Jez: You're delusional, Sal. You may have your little minions, but let's not forget the legion I can call on at anytime. Cyn needs to move on from you and your destructive ways.

She leans in and whispers to Sal, "You're in my way."

Sal *(backs up and responds)*: You're the one

who's destructive, Jez. You're just trying to assert your dominance over me.

Jez: I don't need to assert anything, Sal. I am the more powerful spirit, and Cyn needs to be free of your negative influence.

Sal: You're just trying to take my place, Jez. Well, it's not going to happen. Cyn is mine, and I won't let you have her.

Jez: Sal, Cyn has dealt with you for too long. There is not enough space in this house for both of us.

Sal: How dare you! You think you're so superior, but you're just a jealous rival.

Jez: I'm not jealous, Sal. I just want what's best for Cyn. And that means getting rid of you.

Sal: You'll regret this, Jez. I won't forget how you've betrayed me.

Jez: I haven't betrayed you, Sal. I'm just doing

what needs to be done. And I won't let you stand in the way of Cyn's happiness.

"Happiness? Why does Jez care about Cyn's happiness?" Sal thinks to himself.

Sal: Come on, Pete. Let's get out of here.

Pete: Wait, what's going on? Why are you leaving so suddenly?

Sal: It's none of your business, Pete. I just need to get away from here.

Pete: But I thought we were friends. You can tell me what's going on.

Sal: Not this time, Pete. I need to deal with this on my own.

Pete: Deal with what? Is it something to do with Cyn?

Sal: It's none of your concern, Pete. I just need to leave.

Pete: Fine, but if you ever need to talk or if there's anything I can do to help, you know where to find me.

Sal: I appreciate that, Pete. But right now, I just need to be alone.

Sal leaves with a heavy heart, feeling betrayed by Jez and angry at the situation. He knows that he needs to move on from Cyn, but it's hard to let go of someone he's been with for so long. As he walks away, he can feel the weight of his past bearing down on him, and he wonders what the future holds. Despite his uncertainty, he knows that he needs to find a way to move forward and start a new chapter in his life.

Red is a powerful spirit who has inhabited the control room, also known as the mood room, for as long as anyone can remember. He is known for his unwavering strength and his ability to control the emotions of those around him.

For the past few days, Red has been keeping a close eye on Sal, Pete, and Jez as they navigate their way through their daily lives. Sal and Pete are two best friends who have been inseparable since childhood, but lately, their dynamic has been disrupted by the presence of Jez.

Red has watched as Sal and Pete have struggled to maintain their friendship in the face of Jez's constant meddling. He has seen the frustration and anger build up inside them, and he knows that something needs to be done to restore the balance.

As the spirit of the mood room, Red has the power to influence the emotions of those around him. He decides to use this power to help Sal and Pete overcome their differences and repair their friendship. He begins by subtly altering their moods, making them more open and receptive to each other's perspectives. Over time, Red's influence begins to have a noticeable effect. Sal and Pete start to communicate more openly, and they begin to understand each other's perspectives better. Jez, sensing that she is no longer the center of attention, starts to fade into the background, and the three of them start to become a cohesive unit once again.

Red watches as the three of them laugh and joke together, relieved that his intervention has had the desired effect. He knows that he will always be there, watching over them and using his power to keep their emotions in check. For as long as they need him, Red will be the guardian of the mood room, ensuring that the balance is always maintained.

# CHAPTER 11

## WHERE ARE YOU?

Cyn wakes up to the sound of birds chirping outside her window. She rubs her eyes and looks around her new bedroom. Boxes are stacked up against the wall, waiting to be unpacked. Today is the first day of her new school, and she can't believe she is starting over again. She has never moved before, so this is not something she is used to.

She gets out of bed and walks over to the window. She looks out and sees that the sun is just starting to rise. The sky is a beautiful shade of pink and orange. She takes a deep breath and tells herself that everything is going to be okay. She has to remind herself that she is strong.

Cyn starts to unpack her clothes and put them away in her new closet. She tries to make her new room feel as homey as possible. She hangs up some pictures of her family and friends, and she even puts up some fairy lights around her bed. She wants to make this new house feel like a home.

After she finishes unpacking, Cyn makes herself some breakfast and gets ready for her first day at her new school. She puts on her favorite outfit and takes one last look in the mirror. She feels good about how she looks, but she can't shake the feeling of anxiety that is building up inside her.

Cyn walks to her new school with a knot in her stomach. She doesn't know anyone, and she is afraid of being alone. She takes a deep breath and walks through the front doors of the school. She sees groups of students hanging out in the hallways, and she feels even more nervous. She doesn't know where to go or who to talk to.

As she walks down the hallway, she hears someone call her name. She turns around and sees a girl smiling at her. "Hi, I'm Kaylan," the girl says. "I saw you walking by yourself, and I thought I'd say hi."

Cyn smiles back at Kaylan, feeling relieved. They start talking and Cyn realizes that Kaylan is a lot like her. She had also moved to this school recently and was looking to make new friends. They walk to their first class together, and Cyn feels like she has made a new friend. Throughout the day, Cyn meets more people and it feels like she is making more friends. She finds that people are friendly and welcoming. She even joins a few clubs and signs up for some after-school activities. By the end of the day, Cyn is exhausted but happy. She has survived her first day at her new school, and she has made some new friends.

As Cyn walks back to her new house, she feels grateful. She had worried so much about starting over again, but she has found that people are kind and welcoming. She realizes that moving has its challenges, but it also has its rewards. She has a new home, new friends, and a new beginning. But things are still the same as it relates to her family.

As Cyn walks through the door, she sees her mom, Ruth, surrounded by boxes, unpacking and talking on the phone with her friends.

"Hey, Mom," Cyn says, trying to sound cheerful. Ruth turns and smiles, "Hey, sweetie! How was your first day?"

"It was okay," Cyn replies, trying not to sound too down.

Ruth senses her daughter's mood. "What's wrong, Cyn?"

Cyn sighs, "I just don't know anyone, and it was hard trying to make friends. Plus, the classes were really hard."

Ruth puts down the box she is holding and walks over to her daughter, "I know it's hard, but you'll make friends eventually. And as for the classes, don't worry; you'll get the hang of it."

Cyn nods. "I hope so."

Ruth hugs her daughter. "Just remember, we're here for you. And speaking of that, I was just talking to my friends about going to a new church. Would you like to come with us this Sunday?"

Cyn thinks for a moment. "Sure, why not? It could be a good way to meet new people."

Ruth smiles, "Great! I think you'll like it there."

As they continue unpacking, Ruth fills Cyn in on the details of the new church that they will be attending. It was a large, welcoming community, and Ruth is excited about the prospect of making new friends there.

Over the next few days, Cyn tries to adjust to her new school and surroundings. She finds that the classes are indeed challenging, but she is determined to do her best. She also tries to make friends, but it isn't easy. Initially, they'd welcomed her, but now, the children seem to be a little more distant. Most of the kids seem to already have their own friend-groups, and Cyn feels like an outsider.

On Sunday, Cyn and Ruth get dressed up and head to the new church. As soon as they arrive, they are greeted by friendly faces and warm welcomes. Cyn feels a glimmer of hope. Maybe this can be the start of something new.

The service is uplifting, and the people are kind. Cyn finds herself enjoying it more than she expected. After the service, Ruth introduces her to some of the other families, and Cyn feels a sense of belonging she hasn't felt since they moved.

As they leave the church, Cyn turns to Ruth and says, "Thanks for bringing me here, Ma. I really liked it."

Ruth smiles, "Aww, Bookie. Maybe we can come back next week?"

Cyn nods, feeling more optimistic than she has in days. As they walk back to their new home, she feels a sense of excitement about what the future might hold. Maybe this new place won't be so bad after all.

Over the next few weeks, Cyn finds herself looking forward to going to the new church every Sunday. She has made some new friends there, and she finally feels like she is starting to fit in. She also starts to feel more comfortable at school as she gets used to the routine and the expectations of her new teachers.

One day, Cyn's English teacher announces that they will be doing a group project. Cyn feels a twinge of anxiety because she has never been good at working in groups. But to her surprise, her teacher assigns her to work with two other girls: Mia and Kaylan. They seem nice enough, but Cyn is still nervous about working with them. She does remember Kaylan from her first day at the school. They'd clicked so well, but Cyn still has her guard up.

As they start to plan their project, Cyn finds that Mia and Kaylan are actually really cool. They are smart and creative, and they listen to her ideas. Cyn starts to feel like she has potentially found some real friends at her new school.

After a few weeks of working together, the group project is finally finished. Cyn feels proud of what they have accomplished together, and she's grateful for the opportunity to work with Mia and Kaylan. She realizes that sometimes, good things can and do come out of unexpected situations.

As Cyn and Ruth drive home from church one Sunday, Ruth turns to her daughter, and says, "You know, baby, I'm really proud of you. You've been so brave and resilient since we moved here. I know it hasn't been easy, but you've really made the best of it."
Cyn smiles, feeling a sense of warmth and appreciation for her mom. "Thanks, Ma. I couldn't have done it without you."
Ruth grins, "Well, you know what they say—the apple doesn't fall far from the tree."

Cyn laughs, feeling grateful for her mom's sense of humor and support. As they pull into the driveway of their new home, Cyn feels a sense of contentment that she hasn't felt since they moved. Maybe this new place isn't so bad after all.

Cyn seems to be happy and full of gratitude as

of now, but her mood seems to flicker in this particular season of her life. Hopefully, the next day will be just as good.

As Cyn and Ruth walk into their new home, Cyn turns to her mother and says, "Ma, can I ask you something?"
"Sure, Bookie" Ruth replies.
"So, there are two girls at school that I have been hanging out with named Kaylan and Mia. They invited me to their birthday party next weekend, and I was wondering if I can go."
Ruth smiles, "Of course, you can, Cyn! I'm so glad you're making friends here."

Cyn grins, feeling confused, yet excited at the prospect of attending her first social event in this new place. The confusion lies in the fact that her mom is being so nice about it.
"Thanks, Ma. I can't wait."

The next week flies by quickly. Cyn lets Kaylan and Mia know that she will be attending their party. They are very excited that she can come. Before Cyn knows it, it is the day of the party.

She has spent the entire week thinking about what to wear and what kind of gift to bring. She settles on a cute dress and a couple of gift cards for the duo from a local bookstore.

As Ruth drops her off at the party, Cyn feels a mix of nervousness and excitement. She takes a deep breath and walks up to the door where Kaylan and Mia greet her with big smiles.

The party is everything Cyn hoped it would be. It comes complete with a cake, music, and games, and Cyn feels like she is finally starting to fit in with this new group of friends. She chats with Kaylan and Mia, as well as some of the other girls from school. She even got up to dance a few times.

As the party starts to wind down, Cyn feels a sense of happiness and contentment. She realizes that, despite the challenges of moving to a new place, she has managed to make some new friends and create some good memories. She is grateful for her mom's support and for the opportunities that have come her way.

As Ruth picks her up from the party, Cyn can't seem to stop talking about how much fun she had. "Thanks for letting me go, Mom! I had so much fun!"

Ruth smiles, "I'm so glad, baby. You deserve to have tons of fun and make some new friends."

Cyn nods, feeling grateful and content. She knows that there will still be challenges ahead, but she feels more equipped to face them now that she has some new friends by her side. As they drive home, she looks out at the unfamiliar landscape and feels a sense of hope for the future.

As they pull into the driveway of their new home, Cyn's phone buzzes in her pocket. She pulls it out to see a message from the group chat with Kaylan and Mia. It reads, "OMG! Cyn, that guy from the party was asking for your number! You should give it to him ;)!"

Cyn's heart skips a beat. She had noticed the guy at the party. He was cute and they had chatted a bit, but she hadn't expected him to

be interested in her. She feels a mix of excitement and nervousness as she types out a response: "What should I do??"
Kaylan replies almost instantly, "Give him your number! You're single and ready to mingle, girl."

Cyn blushes, feeling both flattered and embarrassed. She isn't used to this kind of attention from guys, and the idea of giving out her number makes her feel vulnerable.
But then she thinks about all the changes she has gone through in the past few weeks—moving to a new place, starting at a new school, making new friends. She realizes that she has been so focused on trying to fit in and navigate this new environment that she hasn't allowed herself to have any fun or take any risks.

Cyn takes a deep breath and types out her response. "Okay, I'll do it," she says.
Kaylan and Mia reply with a flurry of excited emojis and encouraging messages. Cyn can't help but smile at their enthusiasm.

As she gets ready for bed that night, Cyn feels a sense of anticipation and excitement. She has given the guy her number, and now she is just waiting to see what happens. She realizes that, even though there are still challenges ahead, she is starting to feel more at home in this new place. She is grateful for her new friends, her supportive mom, and for the opportunities that lie ahead.

Cyn puts her phone on the charger and settles into bed, feeling great that she has given Shane her number.

The next day, Cyn wakes up to a text from Shane. He texted her to say that he'd had a great time talking to her at the party and that he would like to hang out with her sometime. Cyn's heart flutters with excitement as she reads the message. She quickly replies and they make plans to hang out after church on Sunday.

Cyn is eager to see Shane again, but she also wants him to get to know more about her life, so she invites him to come to her church with her. She lets him know that they can grab lunch or coffee afterward.

Sunday arrives, and Cyn and Shane meet up at her church. Cyn is happy to see him and introduces him to some of her new friends. They sit together during the service, and afterward, they go to a nearby coffee shop for lunch.

As they sip their coffee, they talk about their interests, families, and their plans for the future. Cyn feels a sense of ease around Shane and realizes that she is really enjoying his company. After lunch, they go for a walk in the park nearby. They laugh and joke around, enjoying the warm sunshine and the sound of birds chirping. Cyn feels like she has made a real connection with Shane; she is excited to see where things will potentially go.

However, as the sun begins to set, Cyn realizes that she needs to get home soon. She looks at her watch and realizes that she has lost track of time. She quickly says goodbye to Shane and begins to make her way home.

However, as Cyn walks home, she starts to feel uneasy. She has never been in this part of town before, and it is getting dark. She looks around nervously, trying to find her bearings.

Suddenly, Cyn realizes that she is lost. She doesn't recognize any of the streets, and she can't seem to remember how to get back to her new home. She starts to panic, feeling her heart racing with fear.

Cyn tries to retrace her steps, but everything looks the same. She doesn't have her phone with her, so she can't call anyone for help. She feels completely alone and vulnerable.

Meanwhile, back at home, Ruth is starting to worry. Cyn had left with Shane hours ago, and she hasn't heard from her since. She tries calling Cyn's phone, but it goes straight to voicemail. Ruth feels a sense of panic rising in her chest.

She decides to go out and look for Cyn. She drives around the neighborhood, calling out her name. She even asks a few people if they have seen her, but there is no sign of Cyn anywhere.

As the hours pass, Ruth's worry turns to desperation. She calls the police and reports her daughter missing. She doesn't know what else to do.

Finally, as the sun begins to rise, Cyn stumbles upon a gas station. She walks inside and asks the clerk for help. The clerk calls the police, who arrive soon after.

Cyn is safe, but she is traumatized by her experience. She has never felt so scared and alone in her life. When Ruth arrives at the gas station, she hugs her daughter tightly, feeling grateful that she is alive and unharmed.

From that day forward, Cyn and Ruth are even more cautious about making sure they know where each other are and that they have a way to contact one another. They also talk about the importance of staying safe in unfamiliar surroundings.

Despite the scary experience, Cyn is grateful for the kindness and concern of the people who helped her. She realizes that, even in this new and unfamiliar place, there are still good people who care about her well-being. She vows to always stay safe and never take her safety for granted again; that is until her and Ruth start disagreeing about going to other places without her mom accompanying her. Ruth has turned over a new leaf with Cyn since they moved. Ruth used to be very angry and emotionally abusive. Cyn is happy that Ruth is spending time with God and recognizing her gifts and purpose. Let's hope these two keep things at peace afterwards.

## CHAPTER 12

# WHO IS IN THE HOUSE?

*A stronghold spirit and the Jezebel spirit are two distinct spirits that are assigned to silence Prophets. A stronghold refers to a mental or spiritual obstacle that prevents a person from experiencing the fullness of God's love and power in their life. It could be a negative belief system, an addiction, or any thought pattern that hinders a person's spiritual growth. Breaking a stronghold requires a deliberate effort to replace negative thoughts with positive ones and to renew one's mind with the truth of God's Word.*

*On the other hand, the Jezebel spirit is a term used to describe a demonic influence that operates through people to control, manipulate, and dominate others. It's named after Jezebel, the wife of King Ahab in the Old*

*Testament, who was known for her idolatry and wickedness. The Jezebel spirit manifests through people who exhibit traits such as pride, deception, intimidation, and a desire for power and control. Its goal is to disrupt relationships, sow discord, and create chaos.*

*While both strongholds and the Jezebel spirit are spiritual concepts, they operate in different ways. A stronghold is an internal obstacle that affects an individual's relationship with God, while the Jezebel spirit is an external force that seeks to control and manipulate others. Overcoming a stronghold requires an individual effort to replace negative thoughts with positive ones, while dealing with the Jezebel spirit may require prayer, deliverance, and sometimes confrontation or fasting.*

As Pete and Sal keep a close eye on Jez, Lacy and Charlotte, Pete's daughters, come in from the kitchen to check on their father. They can see that something is amiss, as their father seems troubled.

"Is everything alright, Dad?" Lacy asks, looking

at her father with concern.

Pete shakes his head. "No, everything's not alright. There's a new spirit in the house, and she's causing trouble."

Charlotte chimes in. "Who is she? What's she doing?"

Pete sighs. "Her name is Jez, and she's a Jezebel spirit. She's been manipulating the other spirits and causing chaos in the house. We're trying to keep an eye on her, but it's not easy."

As they are speaking, there is a knock on the door. It is Red, the stronghold of the house, who controls everything from the mood room. He sees Jez and instantly confronts her about being in the mood room and changing things around.

"What are you doing in the mood room, Jez?" Red demands, his eyes blazing with anger.

Jez smirks. "Just trying to liven things up around here. You know how it is, Red. Sometimes, the spirits need a little more excitement."

Red isn't amused. "I don't appreciate you changing things without my permission. This is my house, and I make the rules. If you can't follow them, then you're not welcome here." Jez shrugs. "Suit yourself, Red. I can take care of myself. But just remember, I know things about this house that you don't. And I can make things very interesting around here if I want to."

With that, Jez disappears, leaving the other spirits feeling uneasy. They know that Jez is up to something, and they have to be careful around her, but they also know that they can't let her control their actions and emotions. Pete and Sal look at each other, knowing that they will have to work together to protect the house from Jez's wicked ways. They know that it won't be easy, but they are determined to keep the peace in the house and prevent Jez from causing any more trouble.

As the days pass, Jez continues to cause chaos in the house. She whispers lies and manipulates the other spirits, causing them to doubt their beliefs and values. Pete, Sal, Lucy, and Charlotte know that they have to do something to stop Jez before she causes irreversible damage to the house.

One day, they gather all the spirits in the house and have a meeting to discuss Jez's behavior. They all share their concerns and talk about how Jez's actions are affecting their work with Cyn. They realize that they need to confront Jez and ask her to leave the house.

As they were discussing Jez, she walks into the room with a sly smile on her face. "What's going on, guys?" she asks innocently.
Pete steps forward. "Jez, we need to talk to you. Your behavior in the house is causing chaos and confusion. We can't let you continue to manipulate and deceive us."
Jez laughs. "Oh, come on, Pete. What's the harm in a little fun? I'm just trying to spice things up around here."
Sal speaks up. "It's not just about fun for you, Jez. Your actions are affecting our fun and our assignments. We can't let you continue to

disrupt the peace in the house."

Jez's expression turns dark. "You think you can tell me what to do? I don't answer to anyone. I'll do what I want, when I want."

Red steps forward, his eyes flashing with anger. "That's where you're wrong, Jez. You may be a Jezebel spirit, but this is my house, and I make the rules. If you can't abide by them, then you need to leave."

Jez and Red continue to stare each other down, each unwilling to back down. Suddenly, the entire house starts shaking violently as if an earthquake has hit. Things are flying around the house, and the spirits are struggling to keep their balance.

Red knows that something is terribly wrong. He has to make it to the mood room to figure out what is happening. He fights his way through the chaos and finally makes it to the mood room where he can see what Cyn is doing. Of course, Cyn is the person who's hosting the spirits, and it is her mood that he is tasked to control.

As he looks into the mood room, Red can see that Cyn is in a state of panic. She is frantically searching for something, moving things around in her house, and throwing things around in a fit of rage. The more she panics, the more the spiritual house shakes.

Red realizes that Cyn's emotions are affecting the spiritual realm, causing chaos and destruction. He knows that he has to calm her down, but he doesn't know how. As he watches, a beam of light appears in the mood room. It is Cyn's angels. They can see that Cyn is reaching out for help. Red knows that he has to act fast.

Just as the house is returning to a state of calm, a blinding light fills the room. Everyone shields their eyes as the light grows brighter and brighter until it is all they can see.

As the light fades, figures begin to emerge from within it. They are Cyn's angels, sent to protect her from the demonic spirits that are trying to control her.

The angels' light is so bright that it blinds all of the demonic spirits in the room, except for Jez and Red. Jez is still seething with rage, but even she is taken aback by the power of the angels. Red, on the other hand, feels a sense of relief wash over him. He knows that the angels have a fighting chance against Jez and her minions. However, he also knows that he and Jez will have to put aside their differences and work together if they want to stand a chance against the angels.

"We may not like each other," Red says to Jez, "....but we need to put our differences aside for now. We have a common enemy, and we need to work together to defeat them."
Jez sneers at him. "I don't need your help, Red. I can handle the angels on my own."

But Red knows better. He has seen the power of angels in action, and he knows that they need to work together if they want to win.

Together, they rally the spirits and form a plan of attack. They know that they will have to be strategic if they want to take down the angels.

As the angels descend upon them, Jez and Red lead the charge, using their powers to strike at the angels' weaknesses. The battle is fierce, with both sides giving it their all.

But in the end, it was the unity and teamwork of the spirits that won the day. Together, they were able to overcome the angels and protect Cyn from their influence.

As the angels retreat into the light from which they came, Jez and Red look at each other, each silently acknowledging the other's contribution to their victory.

But the house is empty. There is no sound or any others in sight. Red and Jez have no worries.

"They will be back." someone says.

# DELIVERANCE IS THE CHILDREN'S BREAD

*Deliverance is a concept that is central to the Christian faith. It refers to the process of being set free from spiritual oppression, bondage, and the power of sin. The Bible teaches that all people are born into sin and that the only way to be delivered from this bondage is through faith in Jesus Christ.*

*The first step in the process of deliverance is recognizing that we need it. The Bible tells us that all have sinned and fallen short of the glory of God (Romans 3:23). This means that we are all in need of salvation and deliverance from the power of sin.*

*The second step is repentance. Repentance involves acknowledging our sinfulness, confessing our sins to God, and turning away from our sinful ways. The Bible tells us that if we confess our sins, God is faithful and just to forgive us our sins and to cleanse us from all unrighteousness (1 John 1:9).*

*The third step is accepting Jesus Christ as our Lord and Savior. The Bible teaches that salvation is found in no one else but Jesus (Acts 4:12). By* believing in Jesus and accepting Him as our Savior, we are delivered from the power of sin and given new life in Christ (Romans 6:23).

Once we have been delivered from the power of sin through faith in Jesus Christ, we are called to live a life that is pleasing to God. This involves walking in obedience to His commands, seeking His will for our lives, and relying on His strength to resist temptation and overcome the power of sin.

In addition to personal deliverance, the Bible also teaches that believers have the power to participate in the deliverance of others. This involves praying for and with others who are struggling with spiritual oppression, sharing the gospel with those who have not yet accepted Jesus Christ, and standing in the gap for those who are unable to fight for themselves.

Deliverance involves recognizing our need for salvation and repenting of our sins, accepting Jesus Christ as our Lord and Savior, and living a life that is pleasing to God. Through faith in Jesus, we are delivered from the power of sin and given new life in Christ. As believers, we are also called to participate in the deliverance of others through *prayer, sharing the gospel, and standing in the gap for those who are in need.*

# CHAPTER 13

## YOU

Cyn and Ruth sit in their living room, their silence only broken by occasional sniffles and tears. The tension in the room is palpable, and both of them are struggling to find the right words to say.

Cyn feels angry and hurt. She feels like her mother is being overprotective and controlling, and she doesn't understand why Ruth has to be so mean to her. She feels like she can't do anything right and that her mother doesn't trust her.

Ruth, on the other hand, feels like she is just trying to protect her daughter. She is scared and worried about what has happened to Cyn, and she doesn't want any more harm to come to her daughter. She feels like she is doing what any good mother would do.

As they sit there, Andre, Cyn's older brother, walks into the room. He can feel the tension immediately and tries to diffuse the situation.

"Hey, what's going on? Why are you guys so upset?" he asks.

Cyn explains what has happened and how she feels like their mother is being overprotective and mean. Ruth tries to defend herself, saying that she is just trying to keep her daughter safe.

Andre listens to both sides and then suggests that they take a break and cool down. He suggests that they all go out for dinner and talk things through calmly. Ruth and Cyn agree, and they head out to a nearby restaurant.

At the restaurant, Ruth, Cyn, and Andre sit down at a booth and order their food. The conversation is awkward at first, but Andre starts it off.

"So, what's been going on? I heard that there was some drama earlier," he says.

Cyn looks at her mother and takes a deep breath before speaking up. "Ma, I just want you to know that I understand you're worried about me, but you can't treat me like a kid anymore. I'm growing up and I need to make my own decisions."

Ruth sighs and rolls her eyes. "I know, Cyn. I just worry about you. I don't want anything bad to happen to you. You are only 16-years old."

"I know, but you have to trust me. I'm not a little kid anymore," Cyn says.

Ruth nods. "I understand, and I'm sorry if I came across as mean or controlling. It's just that I care and love you so much."

Cyn softens a bit. "I know you do, Ma, and I love you too. But I need you to trust me and let me make my own choices."

Andre chimes in. "I think what Cyn is trying to say is that she wants to be able to make her own mistakes and learn from them. That's part of growing up."

Ruth nods. "Okay, I understand. I'll try to give you more space and freedom, but you also have to promise to be careful and stay safe. I'm still traumatized from the last incident. In truth,

I'm terrified."

Cyn smiles. "I promise, Mom."

They finish their meal, feeling a bit more at ease with each other. As they walk out of the restaurant, Ruth puts her arm around Cyn's shoulder.

"I love you, Bookie," she says.

"I love you too, Ma," Cyn replies, feeling grateful for the support of her family.

After dinner, Cyn decides to head out to Kaylan's house to go to a youth service. She feels like she needs some time to herself and some space to think. Ruth agrees, feeling grateful that her daughter is still willing to talk to her after their argument.

As Cyn walks out the door, she feels like things are starting to get better. She is still shaken by what happened, but she knows that she has a loving family who cares about her. She vows to communicate better with her mother and to always stay safe when she is out and about.

Meanwhile, Ruth sits at home, feeling grateful that her family is back on track. She realizes that she needs to find a balance between being protective and giving her daughter room to grow.

After leaving the restaurant, Cyn goes straight to Kaylan's house for the youth service. As soon as she walks into the building, she feels a sense of peace and comfort. The atmosphere is filled with music, laughter, and the Spirit of God.

As the worship begins, Cyn feels her heart begin to overflow with emotions. She sings and worships her heart out, feeling a sense of connection with God that she has never felt before. She closes her eyes and allows herself to fully surrender to the moment.

Suddenly, she feels a hand on her shoulder. She opens her eyes to see a woman she has never met before. The woman has a kind and gentle face, and she smiles at Cyn.

"God has a special plan for you, my dear," the woman whispers in Cyn's ear. "He's releasing your gifts and shaping you into a wonderful woman of God."

Cyn's eyes fill with tears as the woman continues to pray over her. She feels the presence of God surrounding her, and she knows that this is a moment she will never forget.

As the worship continues, Cyn falls to the floor, with tears streaming down her face. She feels a deep sense of peace and joy, knowing that God has a plan for her life. She prays and thanks God for the moment, feeling grateful for the love and support of the people around her.

After the service ends, Cyn walks out of the building feeling a sense of hope and excitement for the future. She knows that her life is going to be different from now on, and she is ready for whatever God has in store for her.

As Cyn walks out of the youth service, still feeling the weight of the emotional encounter she just had, the woman who had prayed over her rushes to catch up with her.

"Excuse me," the woman says, "I'm sorry to bother you, but I feel like God gave me a message for you."

Cyn turns to face the woman and sees the same kind and gentle smile on her face she'd had during service.

"Okay," Cyn says, "I'm listening."

The woman takes a deep breath and begins to speak. "God has shown me that you have a prophetic gift, my dear. He wants to use you to speak His Word to others."

Cyn feels her heart skip a beat. She has never heard anything like this before, but as the woman continues to speak, her words become more and more specific.

"I see that you've recently moved to this area, and you've been struggling to adjust. But God wants you to know that He has a plan for you here. He's going to use you to touch many lives, and you will find a sense of purpose that you've been searching for."

Cyn's eyes widen as the woman speaks. She has never met this woman before, and yet she seems to know so much about her.

The woman continues, "God wants you to know that He sees your heart, and He's going to use your gifts to bring healing to others. Don't be afraid to step out in faith and trust Him. He's going to give you the strength and courage you need to fulfill His plan for your life."

Cyn feels a sense of peace wash over her. She knows that the woman's words are true and that God has a special plan for her. She thanks the woman for her message and walks away, feeling grateful and blessed.

As she walks home, Cyn can't help but think about the woman's words. She knows that she has a lot to learn and a long way to go, but she is excited for the journey ahead. She is ready to step out in faith and trust God with her future.

Cyn walks into the house, feeling a sense of calm and peace. As she closes the door behind her, she knows that she has to share what has happened at the youth service with her mother, Ruth. She finds Ruth in the living room, reading her Bible.

"Mom, can we talk?" Cyn asks, her voice barely above a whisper.

Ruth looks up from her Bible and sees the expression on Cyn's face. She instantly knows that something is different.

"Of course, baby," Ruth says, putting her Bible down. "What's on your mind?"

Cyn takes a deep breath and begins to tell Ruth about her encounter with the woman at the youth service. As she speaks, she can see the expression on Ruth's face change from curiosity to amazement.

After Cyn finishes her testimony, Ruth asks, "Do you want us to pray together right now?"

Cyn nods, and they both kneel down on the living room floor. As they pray, the presence of God fills the house, and both Cyn and Ruth begin to weep. Suddenly, Cyn starts to go through deliverance.

Ruth is shocked and scared, not knowing what to do. She immediately calls some of her friends from the church who are experienced in the ministry of deliverance to come over and help.

As Cyn and Ruth continue to pray, the presence of God begins to swell in the room. Cyn closes her eyes and focuses on God, but without warning, she begins to feel all the more uncomfortable, like something inside her is fighting against the prayer.

She starts to manifest rejection, screaming out words like, "No one loves me!" and "I'm not good enough!" Ruth is shocked to see her daughter in this state, but she knows that this is just the beginning.

Cyn's body begins to contort and writhe

around on the floor as she manifests other things like perversion and lust. Ruth and her friends continue to pray over her, speaking truth and life into her.

It is a difficult and painful process for Cyn, but she knows that she has to go through it in order to be set free. She cries out in agony as the darkness inside her is exposed and expelled.

Finally, after what feels like hours, Cyn's body goes limp. As she lies on the floor, exhausted but at peace, Ruth and her friends continue to pray over her, speaking words of healing and wholeness.

Cyn slowly opens her eyes, and looks up at her mother with tears streaming down her face. "Thank you, Mom," she whispers. "Thank you for being there for me."

Ruth hugs her tightly, feeling grateful and relieved that her daughter has been set free. "I love you, Cyn," she says. "I'm so proud of you."

As they both stand up, Cyn knows that her life will never be the same again. She has been delivered from the spiritual oppression that has been holding her back, and she is ready to step out in faith and trust God with her future.

It took hours upon hours, but finally, Cyn is delivered from the spiritual oppression that has been holding her back. Ruth and her friends pray over her and speak words of life and truth into her.

When it is over, Cyn feels a weight lift off her shoulders. She knows that she has been set free, and that God has a plan for her life.

"Thank you, Mom," Cyn says once again with tears streaming down her face. "Thank you for being there for me."

As Cyn and Ruth stand up from the floor, they both think that everything is over. They are both exhausted, but at the same time, they feel like they have just taken the first steps towards freedom.

However, as they are walking towards the kitchen to get some water, they both start to manifest. This time, it was even more intense than before. Ruth feels a wave of panic wash over her. She has never experienced anything like this in her life.

Their friends call the pastor from their church, and he rushes over to their house. As soon as he arrives, he can see that something is wrong.

The manifestations are getting more and more intense, and Cyn and Ruth are both struggling to stay on their feet. The pastor knows that he has to act quickly to bring them both back into a place of peace.

He begins to pray over them, calling out to God to intervene and bring healing to their bodies, souls, and spirits. He speaks words of truth and life, commanding the darkness to leave and the light of Christ to come in.

As the prayer continues, Cyn and Ruth begin to calm down. The manifestations slowly subside, and they both fall to their knees with tears streaming down their faces.

It was a difficult and intense experience, but they both know that they have come out on the other side stronger than before. They'd faced their demons head-on and come out victorious.

As the pastor hugs them both, they feel a sense of peace wash over them. They know that they have a long journey ahead of them, but with God by their side, they can face anything.

From that day forward, Cyn and Ruth continue to pray together every night, seeking God's wisdom and guidance for their lives. They know that they will face more challenges in the future, but they also know that they have the strength and courage to overcome them.

The more they pray and read their Bibles, the more Cyn starts to experience a lot of prophetic dreams, angelic encounters, and words from the Holy Spirit.

Fast-forward ten years later, and Cyn has grown into a strong, independent woman. She has become a successful business owner, plus, she oversees a thriving ministry that helps women who have experienced trauma and abuse.

However, one night, Cyn finds herself in the midst of a demonic encounter. She is paralyzed with fear as she feels the presence of evil surrounding her. It was as if all the demons from her past had come back to haunt her.

But instead of giving in to the fear, Cyn calls on the name of Jesus for help. She prays with all her might, asking for the strength and courage to face this new challenge.

As she prays, she feels a sudden surge of power within her. The presence of God fills her, and she feels like she can take on anything that comes her way.

And just as suddenly as it had come, the

presence of evil dissipates. Cyn is left standing there, trembling, but victorious.

But the challenges don't end there. Her mother, Ruth, has become seriously ill, and Cyn spends months caring for her. It is a difficult and trying time, but Cyn never gives up. She knows that she has to be strong for her mother, just like her mother had been strong for her when she was a child.

And to make matters worse, Cyn's brother, Andre, ends up in jail. It is a devastating blow to the family, and Cyn struggles to understand why this is all happening. She prays constantly for her brother, asking God to protect him and keep him safe.

Through all of these challenges, Cyn never loses her faith. She knows that God is with her, guiding her through the storms of life. And even though the road ahead will prove to be difficult, she is determined to keep moving forward, trusting in God's plan for her life.

## *IT'S NOT THE END.......*

*Spiritual moments can happen at any time, in any place, and they often come unexpectedly. They are those moments that leave us feeling connected to God, and we may not always know how to process them. However, it is through these moments that the Holy Spirit can enter our lives and guide us towards a deeper understanding of our faith.*

*As believers, it is our responsibility to seek these moments and allow the Holy Spirit to guide us. In John 16:13, Jesus tells His disciples, "When the Spirit of truth comes, he will guide you into all the truth, for he will not speak on his own authority, but whatever he hears he will speak, and he will declare to you the things that are to come." This verse reminds us that the Holy Spirit is a guide, and it is our responsibility to listen and follow His lead.*

*When we allow the Holy Spirit to enter our lives, we become more aware of His presence and the spiritual moments that He brings. We begin to see God's work in our lives and the lives of those around us. Galatians 5:25 says, "If we live by the Spirit, let us also keep in step with the Spirit." By keeping in step with the Spirit, we can mature in our faith and make decisions that honor God.*

*However, it is important to remember that we have free will and can choose to ignore the guidance of the Holy Spirit. When we do this, we may miss out on important spiritual moments and opportunities for growth in our faith. In Ephesians 4:30, Paul warns us not to grieve the Holy Spirit by ignoring his guidance and indulging in sinful behavior.*

*Spiritual moments can be powerful and life-changing, but it is our responsibility as believers to mature in our faith and make decisions with the help of the Holy Spirit. By seeking His guidance and following His lead, we can experience a deeper connection with God and a greater understanding of His plan for our lives.*

**YOU ARE THE HOUSE.**